DEATH ON THE CAPE
and Other Stories

Mary Higgins Clark's first novel *Where are the Children?* was an instant bestseller. She lives in the United States and has five children and a host of grand-children.

By the same author

I'll Be Seeing You
All Around the Town
Loves Music, Loves to Dance
The Anastasia Syndrome and Other Stories
While My Pretty One Sleeps
Weep No More, My Lady
Stillwatch
A Cry in the Night
The Cradle Will Fall
A Stranger is Watching
Where are the Children?

DEATH ON THE CAPE
AND OTHER STORIES

MARY HIGGINS CLARK

ARROW

Published by Arrow Books in 1993

10

*Death on the Cape
and Other Stories*

Death on the Cape and Other Stories first published in 1993 by Century,
Random House, 20 Vauxhall Bridge Road, London SW1V 2SA

Plumbing for Willy © 1992 by Mary Higgins Clark
First published in the US in *Family Circle* in 1992
under the title *The Husband Heist*

The Body in the Closet © 1990 by Mary Higgins Clark
First published in the US by *Women's Day* in 1990

Death on the Cape © 1989 by Mary Higgins Clark
First published in the US by *Women's Day* in 1989

That's the Ticket © 1989 by Mary Higgins Clark
First published in the US by Mysterious Press in 1990

Voices in the Coalbin © 1989 by Mary Higgins Clark
First published in the US by Berkley Books in 1990

Beauty Contest at Buckingham Palace © 1961 by Mary Higgins Clark
First published in the US in *The Saturday Evening Post Stories*, 1961

Milk Run © 1958 by Mary Higgins Clark
First published in the US in Extension Magazine in 1958
under the title *Deadline from Paradise*

Stowaway © 1958 by Mary Higgins Clark
First published in the US in Extension Magazine in 1958
under the title *Last Flight from Danubia*

Arrow Books
The Random House Group Limited
20 Vauxhall Bridge Road, London SW1V 2SA

Random House Australia (Pty) Limited
20 Alfred Street, Milsons Point, Sydney, New South Wales 2061, Australia

Random House New Zealand Limited
18 Poland Road, Glenfield, Auckland 10, New Zealand

Random House (Pty) Limited
Endulini, 5a Jubilee Road, Parktown 2193, South Africa

The Random House Group Limited Reg. No. 954009

www.randomhouse.co.uk

ISBN 0 09 928041 8

Papers used by Random House are natural, recyclable products made
from wood grown in sustainable forests. The manufacturing processes
conform to the environmental regulations of the country of origin.

Designed and Filmset by SX Composing Ltd, Rayleigh, Essex
Printed and bound in Denmark by
Nørhaven Paperback, Viborg

Contents

Stowaway

Carol shivered inside her smoke-blue uniform coat and tried to ignore her growing uneasiness. As she glanced around the waiting room of the air terminal she thought that the gaily-dressed peasant dolls in the showcases made an incongruous background for the grim-faced policeman who passed in front of them. The handful of boarding passengers, watching the policeman, were standing together, their eyes full of hatred.

As she walked toward them, one of the passengers was saying: 'The chase is taking too long. The hunters are not pleased.' He turned to Carol, 'How long have you been flying, stewardess?'

'Three years,' Carol answered.

'You look too young for even that length of time. But if you could have seen my country before it was occupied. This room was always full of gaiety. When I returned to America from my last visit, twenty relatives came to see me off. This time no one dared come. It isn't wise to make a public display of one's American connections.'

Carol lowered her voice. 'There are so many more policemen today than usual. Do you know why?'

'A member of the underground has escaped,' he whispered. 'He was spotted near here an hour ago. They'll surely catch him, but I hope I don't see it.'

'We'll be boarding the plane in fifteen minutes,'

Carol answered reassuringly. 'Excuse me, I must see the Captain.'

Tom had just come in from the Operations Office. He nodded when his eyes met hers. Carol wondered how much longer it would be before her heart stopped racing painfully at every glimpse of him, before she stopped being so aware of his splendid tallness in the dark uniform. She reminded herself sternly that it was time she regarded him as just another pilot and not as the man she had loved so dearly.

She spoke to him, her grey eyes veiled, noncommittal. 'You wanted me, Captain?'

Tom's tone was as businesslike as her own. 'I was wondering if you've checked Paul.'

Carol was ashamed to answer that she'd not thought of the purser on the flight since they'd landed in Danubia an hour before. Sick from the effect of booster shots, Paul had stayed in the crew bunk while the plane was refuelled for the return flight to Frankfurt.

'I haven't, Captain. I've been too interested in the hide-and-seek our friends are playing.' She inclined her head in the direction of the police.

Tom nodded. 'I'd hate to be that poor guy when they catch him. They're positive he's on the field somewhere.'

For a moment Tom's voice was familiar, confidential, and Carol looked at him eagerly. But then he became the Captain speaking to the stewardess again. 'Please go aboard and see if Paul needs anything. I'll have the ground rep bring the passengers out.'

'Right, Skipper.' And she walked toward the entrance to the field.

The cold airport seemed desolate in the half darkness of the October evening. Three policemen were entering the plane next to hers. The sight of them made her shiver as she boarded her plane and went forward to find Paul.

He was asleep, so she gently placed another blanket over him and came back to the cabin. Ten minutes more and they'll all be aboard, she thought, checking her watch. She pulled out her hand mirror and ran a comb through the short blonde hair that curled from under her overseas cap.

Just then she realized with a drenching fear that the mirror was reflecting a thin hand grasping the pole of the small open closet behind her seat. *Someone was trying to hide in the tiny recess there!* She glanced frantically out the seat window for help. The police detachment had left the next plane and was heading in her direction.

'Put away that mirror, mademoiselle.' The words were quiet, the English clear, the accent a heavy undertone. She heard the hangers being pushed aside. She whirled and faced a thin boy of about seventeen with heavy blond hair and intelligent blue eyes.

'Please – do not have fear. I will not harm you.' The boy glanced out the window at the rapidly approaching police. 'Is there another way off this plane?'

Carol's fear changed swiftly. It was for him now that the feeling of disaster swept her. His eyes were frightened and he backed away from the window like a trapped animal, beseeching, urgent, his hand stretched toward Carol, his voice imploring: 'If they find me, they will kill me. Where can I hide?'

'I can't hide you,' Carol protested. 'They'll find you when they search the plane, and I can't involve the airline.' She had a clear picture of Tom's face if the police discovered a stowaway on board, especially if she were concealing him.

Feet were ascending the ramp now, heavy shoes clanging on the metal. A loud series of bangs crashed against the closed door.

9

Carol stared in fascination at the boy's eyes, at the black hopelessness in them. Frantically, she glanced around the cabin. Paul's uniform jacket was hanging in the clothes closet. She pulled it out and snatched his hat off the shelf. 'Put these on, quick.'

Hope brightened the boy's face. His fingers raced at the buttons and he stuffed his hair under the cap. The banging at the door was repeated.

Carol's hands were wet, her fingers numb. She shoved the boy into the rear seat, fumbled at the catch of the ship's portfolio, and scattered baggage declarations in his lap. 'Don't open your mouth. If they ask me your name, I'll say Joe Reynolds and pray they don't check the passports.'

Her legs seemed too weak to carry her to the cabin door. As she pulled at the handle, the realization of what she was doing swept over her and she thought how pitifully transparent the boy's disguise was. She wondered if she could possibly keep the police from searching the plane. The handle turned and the door swung open. She blocked the entrance and forced an annoyed tone as she faced the policeman. 'The steward and I are checking our papers. What's the reason for this?'

'Surely you are aware that a search is being made for an escaped traitor. You have no right to hinder the police in its work.'

'*My* work is being hindered. I'll report this to the Captain. You have no right to enter an American plane.'

'We are searching every plane on the field,' the leader snapped. 'Will you step aside? It would be unpleasant to have to force our way in.'

Realizing it was no use to argue, Carol quickly sat on the seat next to the boy, her body shifted towards him, her back shielding him from the direct view of the police. His head was bowed over the papers. In the dim light, his uniform was passable, and the absence of a tie was not noticeable in his hunched position.

Carol pulled some declarations off his lap and said: 'All right Joe, let's get this finished? "Kralik, Walter, six bottles cognac, value thirty dollars. One clock, value – "'

'Who else is aboard?' the leader asked.

'The purser, who's asleep in the crew bunk,' Carol said nervously. 'He's been very ill.'

The inquisitor's gaze passed over 'Joe' without interest. 'No one else? This is the only American plane here. It is the logical one for the traitor to head for.'

The second policeman had checked the lounges, the clothes closet, and the floor under the seats. The third member of the party came back from the flight deck. 'There is only one man there, asleep. He is too old to be our prisoner.'

'He was spotted near here fifteen minutes ago,' the leader snapped. 'He must be somewhere.'

Carol glanced at her watch. One minute to eight. The passengers must be starting across the field. She had to get rid of the police, hide the boy – in one minute.

She stood up, careful to keep her body directly in front of Joe. By glancing out the opposite window, she could see the waiting-room door opening. She said to the leader: 'You've searched the plane. My passengers are about to board. Will you please leave?'

'You seem strangely anxious to be rid of us, stewardess.'

'My paperwork isn't finished. It's difficult to do it while I'm tending the passengers.'

Steps were hurrying up the ramp. A messenger came in and said to the leader, 'Sir, the Commissioner wants an immediate report on the search.'

To Carol's relief, all three policemen scurried out.

The ground representative and passengers were at the foot of the ramp as the policemen descended. The crew were entering the plane through the forward entrance.

'Joe!' Carol called. The boy was out of the seat, crouching in the aisle. Carol pulled him into the tail and pointed to the men's lounge. 'In there. Take off the uniform and don't open the door for anyone except me.'

She stood at the cabin door and forced a smile at the ground rep and passengers. The ground rep handed her the manifest and waited while she greeted the passengers and showed them their seats.

There were six names on the manifest. Five were typed, and the last one, 'Vladimir Karlov', had been written in. Next to it were four letters, 'exco'.

'Extreme courtesy – who's the VIP?' Carol asked the ground rep softly.

'A real big-shot, the Commissioner of Police in Danubia. He's one of their worst butchers, so handle him with kid gloves. He stopped to talk to the searching party about the escaped prisoner.'

The Commissioner – on her flight! Carol felt sick, but as he climbed the ramp she extended her hand, smiling. He was a tall man of about fifty with thin nostrils, tight lips.

'I have been assigned to seat forty-two.'

Carol knew she couldn't let him sit in the rear of the plane. He'd be sure to see 'Joe' when she brought him out of the lounge. 'It's a beautiful flight to Frankfurt,' she said, her smile easy. 'It would be foolish not to sit in front of the wing – '

'I prefer a rear seat,' he said. 'It gives a considerably smoother flight.'

'This hop is one of our smoothest runs. The front seats won't be bumpy and will give you a better view.'

The Commissioner shrugged and followed her down the aisle. She glanced at the manifest and debated whether to seat him with another passenger. If she did, they might start a conversation and he'd be less likely to be looking around when she brought Joe out of the lounge. But then, remembering the passengers' bitter comments about the search, she decided against it, led him to seat three, placed his bag on the overhead rack, and told him to fasten his seatbelt.

The passenger in seat seven got up and started to walk to the rear. Carol caught up to him at the front of the men's lounge. 'Sir, please take your seat. The plane is starting to move.'

The man's face was white, 'Please, stewardess, I may be ill, I get a little frightened at takeoff.'

Carol took his hand and forced him to let go of the doorknob before he realized it was locked. 'I have some pills that will help. Everyone must be in his seat until we're aloft.

After she'd seen him seated, she snapped on the mike. 'Good evening, I am your stewardess, Carol Dowling. Please fasten your seatbelts and don't smoke until the sign over the forward door goes off. Our destination is Frankfurt, our anticipated flight time two hours and five minutes. A light supper will be served shortly. Please don't hesitate to ask for anything you want. A pleasant trip, everyone.'

When she went to the flight deck, the plane had stopped taxiing and the engines were thundering. She bent over Tom. 'Cabin secure, Captain.'

Tom turned so quickly that his hand brushed against her hair. She felt a warm glow from the touch and unconsciously raised her hand to her hair.

'Okay, Carol.'

The engines were racing – it was hard to catch his

words. A year ago he would have looked up at her and his lips would have formed, 'Love you, Carol,' but that was over now. She had an instant of fierce regret that they hadn't somehow made up their quarrel. On sleepless nights, she'd admitted to herself that Tom had tried: he'd made overtures, but she hadn't given an inch. So his attempts at making up had only ended in worse quarrels, and then he'd been stationed in London for six months so they hadn't seen each other. And now they were on a flight together, two polite co-workers giving no hint that things had ever been different.

She started to turn back to the cabin, but Tom motioned her to wait. He nodded to the first officer and the engines became subdued. She felt an immense loneliness when he turned away from her. There had been a few moments on this flight when he'd seemed friendly, warm – moments when it looked as though they might be able to talk things through. But this will finish it, she thought. Even if I can get Joe to Frankfurt, Tom will never forgive me.

'Carol, did you speak to the Commissioner yet?'

'Just when I showed him his seat. He's not very chatty.'

'Take good care of him. He's important. They're talking about closing Danubia to American planes. If he likes the service, it might help a little. I'll send Dick back to give you a hand with dinner once we're aloft.'

'Don't! I mean, it's just a cold supper. With only six passengers, I can manage.'

Back in the cabin, she smiled reassuringly at the man afraid of takeoffs as she passed him. The plane had reached the runway and the crescendo of engines was deafening. All the passengers, including the Commissioner, were staring out the windows. She went back, tapped on the door of the men's lounge and softly called to Joe.

Noiselessly, he slipped out. In the dim light, his thin body seemed more like a shadow than a human creature. She put her lips to his ear. 'The last seat on the right. Get on the floor. I'll throw a blanket over you.'

He moved warily and disappeared into the seat recess. He walks like a cat, Carol thought. Or like a kitten, she amended, remembering the boyish fuzz that had brushed her face.

It was hard to balance in the ascending plane and, steadying herself by one hand on the lounge bulkhead, she took the aisle seat by Joe, flipped a blanket from the overhead rack, and threw it over him, shaking it wide. To a casual glance, the blanket might not seem unusual; to a searching glance, it would be odd that anything so shapeless could make such a thick mound.

She glued her eyes to the sign over the cabin door. FASTEN YOUR SEATBELTS – NO SMOKING: *Attacher vos veintures – ne fumer pas*. While the sign was on, she had a reprieve, a safe island. But when it flashed off she'd have to turn on the bright cabin lights that would make a farce out of Joe's hiding place and let the passengers leave their seats.

For the first time she seriously considered what would happen to her for concealing Joe. She thought about what Tom would say and remembered unhappily his reaction last year, when she'd caused trouble on his ship.

'But Tom,' she'd protested, 'what if I did let that poor kid take her dog out of the crate? She was traveling alone, to be adopted by strangers. It was night and the cabin was dark. No one would have known if that woman hadn't gone over to her and got nipped for her trouble.'

15

And Tom had retorted: 'Carol, maybe someday you'll learn to obey basic rules. That woman was a stockholder and raised Cain in the front office. I took the blame for letting the dog loose because I knew it wouldn't cost me my job. But after seven years with a clean record, I don't like having a reprimand in my brief now.'

She recalled uneasily how she'd flared at him, telling him she was delighted he didn't have a perfect record to live up to any more – that now, maybe, he'd relax and act human – maybe he'd stop treating the company manual like the Bible. It wasn't hard to remember everything they'd said, she'd relived that quarrel so often.

She tried to picture what Charlie Wright, Northern's station manager at Frankfurt, would do. Charlie was a 'company man', too. He liked the planes to arrive and depart on schedule, the passengers to be satisfied. Charlie would definitely be upset at having to report a stowaway to the front office and would undoubtedly suspend her immediately or fire her outright.

Joe's blanket moved slightly and her mind jolted back to the problem of finding a safe hiding place for him. The plane leveled off. As the seatbelt sign died, she rose slowly. Hating to do it, she reached for the switch on the bulkhead and turned the cabin lights from dim to bright.

She started to pass out magazines and newspapers. The man who'd been nervous about takeoff was no longer strained-looking. 'That pill helped a lot, stewardess.' He accepted a newspaper and fumbled for his glasses. 'They must be in my coat.' He got up and started toward the rear.

Carol said numbly, 'Let me get them for you.'

'Not at all.' He was passing Joe's hiding place – Carol following, scarcely breathing. The blanket was glaringly out of place in the tidy cabin. The passenger got his eyeglasses, started back down the aisle and stopped. Carol swiftly reflected that this man was the *neat* type – hadn't he straightened his coat on the hanger, smoothed the edges of his newspaper? In just one second he'd pick up that blanket. He was bending, saying, 'This must have fallen – '

'Oh please!' Carol's hand was on his arm, her grip firm. 'Please don't bother. I'll get it in a minute.' She eased him forward, scolding lightly: 'You're our guest. If the Captain saw me letting you tidy up, he'd drop me out the window.'

The man smiled, but went amiably to his seat.

Carol's eyes searched the cabin hopelessly. The blanket *was* too obvious. Anytime someone went to the rear of the plane Joe could be discovered.

'Magazine, stewardess.'

'Of course.' Carol brought a selection to the passenger seated behind the Commissioner, then walked forward. 'Would you care to see a magazine, Commissioner Karlov?'

The Commissioner's thin fingers were tapping the armrest, his lips pursed in concentration. 'Some piece of information eludes me, stewardess. Something I have been told does not fit in. However – ' he smiled coldly ' – it will come back to me. It always does.' He waved away the magazine. 'Where is the water fountain?'

'I'll get you a glass of water – ' Carol said.

He started to rise. 'Don't bother, please. I detest sitting so long. I'll get it myself.'

The water fountain was opposite the seat where Joe was hiding. The Commissioner was not a naïve observer. He'd be sure to investigate the blanket.

'No!' She blocked the way into the aisle. 'The flight's getting bumpy. The Captain doesn't want the passengers moving.'

The Commissioner looked significantly at the unlighted seatbelt sign. 'If you will let me pass – '

The plane tilted slightly. Carol swayed against the Commissioner, deliberately dropping the magazines. It *was* getting rough.

If she could just stall him, Tom was sure to flash the sign on. The Commissioner, looking exasperated, picked up a few of the magazines.

Still blocking his way, she slowly picked up the others, carefully sorting them by size. Finally, unable to delay any longer, she straightened up. And the seatbelt sign was flashing!

The Commissioner leaned back and studied Carol intently as she went to the tank, drew him a glass of water, and brought it to him. He didn't thank her but instead observed, 'That sign seemed like a direct answer to a plea of yours, stewardess. It must have been important to you that I did not leave my seat.'

Carol felt panic, then anger. He knew something was up and it amused him to watch her squirm. She took his barely touched glass. 'Sir, I'm going to let you in on a trade secret. When we have a very important passenger on board, a mark is made next to his name on the manifest. That symbol means we're to show every courtesy to that person. You're that passenger on this flight and I'm trying to make your trip as pleasant as possible. I'm afraid I'm not succeeding.'

The flight-deck door opened and Tom stepped down. The passengers were all seated near the front half of the cabin. Carol stood by the last one. The odds were that Tom merely wanted to say hello to them. He wouldn't bother going all the way through with no one seated in the back.

Tom welcomed the Commissioner, shook hands with the man behind him, pointed out a cloud bank to the two friends playing checkers. Carol studied his movements with vast aching. Every time she saw him a different memory flashed back. This time it was Memorial Day in Gander and their flight was canceled because of a freak snowstorm. Late that night, she and Tom had had a snowball fight. Tom had looked at his watch and said: 'Do you realize in two minutes it will be June first? I've never kissed a girl in a snowstorm on June first before.' His lips brushed her cheek and were cold, found her mouth and were warm. 'I love you, Carol.' It was the first time he had said it.

Carol swallowed against the hurt and came back to reality. She was standing in the aisle and Tom was before her and Joe was in danger and there was no way out.

'Sure you don't want help with dinner, Carol?' His tone was impersonal but his eyes searched hers. She wondered if he had flashes of remembering too.

'No need,' she said. 'I'll start on it immediately.' It would mean going up to the galley and leaving Joe for anyone to discover, but –

Tom cleared his throat and seemed to search for words: 'How does it feel to be the only woman on board, Carol – '

The words hung in Carol's mind for seconds before their full import sank in. She gazed from passenger to passenger: the Commissioner, the man afraid of takeoffs, the mild fortyish one. the elderly man sleeping, the two friends at checkers. Men, all men. She'd prayed for a hiding place for Joe, and Tom of all people had pointed it out! The ladies' lounge. Perfect. And so simple.

Now, as Tom studied her, she said casually. 'I love being the only woman here, Captain. No competition.'

Tom started to go forward and hesitated. 'Carol, have coffee with me when we get to Frankfurt. We've got to talk.'

It had come. He missed her too. If she said to him now, 'I've discovered a stowaway on board,' it would be so easy. Tom could take the credit and Danubia would be grateful. It might mean Northern's charter being extended and make up to him for last year's trouble. But she couldn't murder Joe even for Tom's love. 'Ask me in Frankfurt if you still want to,' she said.

After Tom had gone back to the flight deck, she returned to the seat beside Joe and studied the passengers swiftly. The checker game was absorbing the two players. The elderly man dozed. The fortyish man watched clouds. The neat one was bent over his newspaper. The Commissioner's head was leaning against the back of the seat. It was too much to hope he was napping. At best he was in deep thought and might not turn around.

She leaned over the blanketed form. 'Joe, you've got to get to the rear of the plane. The ladies' lounge is on the left. Go in and lock the door.'

Just then she met the Commissioner's glance as he turned in his seat. 'Joe, I've got to turn the lights off. When I do, get out of there fast! Do you understand?'

Joe slipped the blanket from his head. His hair was tousled and his eyes blinked in the strong light. He looked like a twelve-year-old roused from a sound sleep. But when his eyes got used to the light, they were the eyes of a man – weary, strained.

His faint nod was all Carol needed to assure her that he understood. She got up. The Commissioner had left his seat and was hurrying toward her.

It took her a second to cross to the light switch and plunge the cabin into darkness. Cries of alarm came from the passengers. Carol made her cries louder than the rest. 'I'm sorry! How stupid of me! I can't seem to find the right switch – '

The click of a door closing – had she heard it or merely wanted to hear it?

'Turn on that light, stewardess.' An icy voice, a rough hand on her arm.

Carol threw the switch and stared into the face of the Commissioner – a face distorted with rage.

'Why?' His voice was furious.

'Why what, sir? I merely intended to turn the microphone on to announce dinner. See – the mike switch is next to the lights.'

The Commissioner studied the panel, uncertainty crossing his face. Carol turned the mike on. 'I hope you're hungry, everybody. I'll serve dinner in minutes, and while you're waiting we'll have a cocktail. Manhattans, martinis, or daiquiris. I'll be right there to get your orders.' She turned to the Commissioner and said respectfully, 'Cocktail, sir?'

'Will you have one with me, stewardess?'

'I can't drink while I'm working.'

'Neither can I.'

What did he mean by that, Carol wondered, passing the cocktail tray. More cat-and-mouse stuff, she decided as she yanked prepared food from the cubbyhole refrigerator in the galley and made up trays. She took special pains with the Commissioner's dinner, folding the linen napkin in creases and pouring the coffee at the last minute to keep it steaming hot.

'Aren't there usually two attendants?' the Commissioner asked as she placed the tray in front of him.

'Yes, but the purser's ill. He's lying down.'

She served the others, poured second coffees, brought trays to the crew. Tom turned over the controls to the first officer and sat at the navigator's table.

21

'I'll be glad when we get to Frankfurt,' he said uneasily. 'With this tail wind, we should be in in half an hour. I've been edgy this whole flight. Something seems wrong, but I can't put my finger on it.' He grinned. 'Maybe I'm just tired and need some of your good coffee, Carol.'

Carol pulled the curtain from the crew bunk up slightly. 'Paul certainly has been asleep a long time.'

'He just woke up and asked me to get his jacket. He wanted to give you a hand. But I made him stay put. He feels rotten.'

Joe's fate was hanging in such delicate balance. If Paul had come back, he'd have seen Joe. If Paul's jacket hadn't been hanging in the cabin, the police would have found Joe. If Tom hadn't said she was the only woman aboard –

'I'll pick up the trays since we've only a half hour to go,' she said.

She started collecting the trays from the passengers, working her way forward. The Commissioner's tray was untouched. He was staring down at it. A premonition warned Carol not to disturb him. She cleared and stacked the other trays. But then her wristwatch told her they'd land in ten minutes. The seatbelt sign came on. She went for the Commissioner's tray. 'Shall I take it, sir? I'm afraid you didn't eat much.'

But the Commissioner stood up. 'You *almost* got away with it, Miss, but I finally realized what's been eluding me. At Danubia the search party said the purser was ill and the stewardess was checking baggage declarations with the steward.' His face turned cruel. 'Why didn't a steward help you with dinner? Because there isn't any.' His fingers dug into Carol's shoulder. 'Our prisoner *did* get on this plane and you've hidden him.'

22

Carol fought rising panic. 'Let me go.'

'He is on board, isn't he? Well, it's not too late. The Captain must take us back to Danubia. A thorough search will be made.'

He pushed her aside and lunged for the door to the flight deck. Carol grasped at his arm but he flung her hand away. The other passengers were on their feet, staring.

Her last hope was these men who with bitterness had watched the search. Would they help?

'Yes, there's an escaped prisoner on board!' she shouted. 'He's a kid you'd love to shoot, but I won't let you do it!'

For a moment, the passengers seemed frozen as they clutched seat backs for support in the sloping plane. Carol, in utter despair, thought they wouldn't help. But then, as though they finally understood what was going on, they lunged forward together. The mild one threw himself against the Commissioner and knocked his hand from the doorknob. A checker-player pinned his arms behind his back. The plane was circling the field, the airport lights level with the window. A faint bump – Frankfurt!

The passengers released the Commissioner as the flight-deck door opened. Tom stood there, angrily taking in the scene. 'Carol, what the devil is going on?'

She went to him, shutting her eyes against the Commissioner's hatred, and against the impact of her words on Tom. She felt sick, drained, 'Captain – ' Her tongue was thick, she could barely form the words ' – Captain, I wish to report a stowaway . . .'

She gratefully sipped steaming coffee in the station manager's office. The past hour was a blur of airport officials, police, photographers. Only vivid was the Commissioner's demand: 'This man is a citizen of my country. He must be returned immediately.' And the station manager's reply: 'This is regrettable, but we must turn the stowaway over to the Bonn government. If his story checks, he'll be granted asylum.'

She stared at her hand where Joe had kissed it before being taken into custody.

He'd said, 'You have given me my life, my future.'

The door opened and Charley Wright, the station manager, walked in, followed by Tom. 'Well, that's that.'

He looked squarely at Carol. 'Proud of yourself? Feeling real heroic and dying to see the morning headlines? "Stewardess hides stowaway in thrilling flight form Danubia." The papers won't print that Northern won't be welcome in Danubia any more and will lose a few million in revenue because of you. As for you, Carol, you can deadhead home and there'll be a hearing in New York, but – you're fired.'

'I expected it. But you've got to understand Tom knew nothing about the stowaway.'

'It's a Captain's business to know what goes on in his plane,' Charley shot back. 'Tom will probably get away with a stiff calldown unless he gets heroic and tries to take the blame for you. I hear from the grapevine he did that once before.'

'That's right,' Carol said. 'He took the blame for me last year and I didn't have the decency to thank him for it.' She looked into Tom's strangely inscrutable face. 'Tom, last year you were furious with me, and rightly so. I was completely wrong. This time, I'm truly sorry for the trouble you'll have over this but I couldn't have done otherwise.'

She turned to Charley, fighting tears. 'If you're finished, I'm going to the hotel. I'm dead.'

He looked at her with some sympathy. 'Carol, unofficially I can understand what you did. Officially – '

She tried to smile. 'Good night.' She went out and started to walk down the stairs.

Tom caught up with her at the landing. 'Look, Carol, let's put the record straight – I'm *glad* the boy got through! You wouldn't be the girl I love if you'd handed him over to those butchers.'

The girl I love . . .

'But thank God you won't be flying on my plane any more. I'd be afraid to sit at the stick wondering what was going on in the cabin.' His arms slipped around her.

'But if you're not on my plane, I wish you'd be there to pick me up at the airport. You can hide spies and dogs and anything you darn please in the back seat. Carol, I'm trying to ask you to marry me.'

Carol looked at him, the splendid tallness of him and the tenderness in his eyes. Then his lips were warm against hers and he was saying again the words she'd wanted so long to hear, 'Love you, Carol.'

The waiting room of the terminal was dim and quiet. After a moment, they started down the stairs toward it, their footsteps echoing ahead.

Milk Run

Where on earth could Dick be? Jen pulled off her overseas-uniform cap and pushed back the damp brunette ringlets that clustered on her forehead. The April sun shone bright and clear; the green water lapped at the land, but it was hot!

Bermuda, she reflected, might be paradise for honeymooners, but for the stewardesses who worked a flight down from New York, served sixty passengers a three-course lunch, laid over fifty minutes at Kindley Field, and prepared a hot dinner on the return trip, Bermuda was nothing but a milk run.

Why had Dick phoned Operations to make sure she hadn't been canceled from this flight? A sense of trouble, foreign to the sunny afternoon, filled her. It couldn't be cast aside even by thinking of the month since Dick had been the lone passenger on her first Bermuda flight. He had griped about his paper sending him down to do a series of articles on the 'honeymoon paradise' and she had griped about being frozen on the honeymoon-paradise run for a month. The next day he'd been at the terminal to meet her flight and he'd been meeting it every day since.

But this was her last Bermuda trip and next week Dick's assignment would be finished – he'd be back in New York, and they'd spend some lovely evenings making up for all the crowded hours at Kindley Field.

What had Dick meant yesterday when he confided he thought he had stumbled onto a really big story?

She felt a hand on her shoulder, turned, and was in Dick's arms. His kiss was urgent, brief, and fierce. 'Jen, darling.' It was the first time he had called her darling, but it seemed right and natural. 'Listen as carefully as you've ever listened in your life because you've got to get this straight. Here – ' he handed her a rolled-up copy of a magazine ' – stuff this in your pocket book and get it to my newspaper tonight. Go to the office, fifth floor, and ask for Bill Ryan, the night editor.'

'Bill Ryan, fifth floor,' Jen replied. 'But – '

Dick cut her short. 'I'll check with Operations. Fifteen minutes after they tell me your flight has landed, I'll call Ryan and tell him what to expect. Jen, I'm putting you in danger, but I can't help it.'

'What danger, Dick?'

He hesitated. 'You've certainly got a right to know. Jen, remember that carrier that vanished at the end of the Korean War? The papers were full of it.'

Jen nodded soberly. 'A boy I knew was on it.'

'That ship was sabotaged. But over seven hundred men escaped and were taken prisoner. Their names, serial numbers, and the prison camps they've been sent to are listed in that magazine. The Reds would kill rather than see that list printed.'

The loudspeaker in the terminal came on. The clear, precise British voice that never seemed hurried requested all passengers to assemble at Gate 2 for Federal Airlines flight 401 nonstop to Idlewild.

The announcement gave Jen a moment to think. How Dick had managed to get this magazine she didn't know, but obviously someone knew he had it – otherwise he'd be taking it to New York himself. 'Do you think you were followed?' she whispered.

Dick started walking her to the gate. 'I may have lost the car that was trailing me, but I don't know how many of them know I have this. I've signed up for the late New York flight to throw them off.'

They stopped at the gate. Dick kissed her quickly, then reached into his wallet and pulled out a ring. 'Jen, they may try to search me somehow. I bought this to give you in New York, but take it now. It will be safer with you.'

Jen stared down at the solitaire diamond set in a narrow platinum band. An engagement ring, five minutes late. When Dick trusted her with the magazine, he had told her he loved her and needed her. 'In a few days I'll make the conventional speech,' he promised. She slipped the ring into an inside pocket of her uniform jacket, put a hand on his shoulder, kissed him, then raced across the field, up the ramp, and onto the plane.

Allan Bates, the purser, was standing by the door ready to close it. 'For Pete's sake, Jen,' he snapped. 'Captain Evans is having a fit. We're two minutes behind schedule. You make the announcements while I give "cabin secure". You'd better not go near the flight deck till the skipper calms down.'

Jen caught her breath, straightened her cap, and turned on the mike. 'Good evening, ladies and gentlemen, and welcome aboard. We are flying nonstop to Idlewild Airport. Our anticipated flight time is three hours and twenty-five minutes. Please fasten your seatbelts and do not smoke until the sign over the galley door goes off. Push the buzzer at your seat any time you want us – and a pleasant trip, everyone.'

She snapped off the mike, pulled the reserved sign off the flight-service seat, and sat down. Allan joined her just before takeoff. He stared out the window as Jen leaned her head back and closed her eyes.

Her shoulderbag dug into her side and she ran her fingers over it, thinking that she'd have to hide the bag immediately. Dick's warning that she might be followed rang in her ears and she tapped Allan's arm. He turned from the window and bent his head to catch her question.

'Did anyone sign for the flight just before takeoff?'

Allan nodded. 'The ground rep first gave me a manifest with eight names. Thirty seconds later, he came tearing out with an amended manifest with three extra pax.' He reached in his pocket. 'Here's a copy.'

Jen's eyes skimmed quickly down the sheet. Two Mr. and Mrs. They would be the honeymoon couples up front. Four women's names. That would be the four ladies traveling together who'd been telling her at the airport what a lovely time they had in Bermuda. And – here they were – the last three names: Hastings, Walter, seat six; Clinton, Andrew, seat nine; Carlson, August, seat eighteen. Jen shut her eyes. If Dick had been followed, someone might have seen him pass the magazine to her. Someone may have signed up for the flight at the last minute to get the magazine back from her. But which one?

Allan touched her arm. 'Sign's off, Jen. Suppose you give the skipper a cup of coffee? I'll pass out the newspapers.'

Jen went forward to the galley, carefully shut the door between it and the cabin. Being in the tiny galley, situated between the cabin and the flight deck, gave her a chance to think. She reasoned that if she hid her purse here, no passenger could possibly get at it without being noticed at once. If she prepared the dinner and Allan did the serving, she'd be able to guard the purse for almost the whole flight. Still, she'd better hide the bag well in case anyone tried to slip in and search for it. She rejected the grocery closets as being too convenient, bent down, and opened the door of the narrow, dark refrigerator.

On the bottom shelf of the refrigerator, almost level with the floor, were rows of various salads. She carefully reached the purse in and wedged it behind them.

Satisfied that it was out of sight, she straightened up and closed the refrigerator door. The satisfaction vanished when she noticed that the oil from one of the salads had made an ugly stain on her sleeve. She dabbed at it with a paper napkin, making it worse, and decided to forget it. Remembering the captain was waiting for coffee, she got out a cup, drew coffee from the tank, shook two lumps of sugar into it, then went forward to the flight deck.

'Hot, sweet, and black, Captain,' she said, trying to make her voice light.

Evans would not respond. He looked at her, his usually pleasant face firm, his eyes cold. 'Jen, I've been flying twenty years and one thing I've never tolerated is a member of my crew holding up a flight. I'm sorry, but I intend to write you up for this. If that was your boyfriend in the terminal, he looks like a nice young fellow, but no matter what he had to say it wasn't important enough to hold up the plane.'

It was important enough, Jen thought, but she said, 'I'm sorry, sir. I didn't realize how late it was.'

Allan was in the galley mixing cocktails when she returned. He thrust a small notebook in which he had scribbled the orders into her hand. 'Finish these up, will you? I'll go back and try to do a little paperwork.'

Jen nodded. Preparing the cocktails would give her a chance to keep a watchful eye on the galley, and serving them would be an opportunity to study the passengers. Especially the latecomers.

She finished making the drinks, went into the cabin, and glanced at the notations Allan had made. Bending over the honeymooners in the first seats, she offered the tray. 'I believe you wanted daiquiris.'

They had been having a low, earnest conversation and looked up startled, 'Oh, thank you.' The girl reached up, colored, and withdrew her hand as her husband took two glasses from the tray and offered her one with a slight ceremony.

Jen smiled. Bermuda might not be a bad place to go if you drank cocktails on the plane instead of serving them, and if you held hands with a brand-new husband. This boy was nice-looking, she thought, but Dick, with his curling brown hair, easy smile, and nonchalant air was much more exciting.

A tap on her shoulder quenched the flow of her happy-ever-after thoughts. The first officer was beside her, saying, 'Jen, the captain says you should send the passengers up to see the flight deck.'

Jen stared at him, dismayed. She'd forgotten that Captain Evans invariably invited the passengers forward. Now every passenger in the plane would go through the galley. But if she finished serving the cocktails at once and made some motions of starting dinner, she could guard the purse while the passengers went through.

The honeymooners stood up eagerly. 'Could we be the first?' the boy asked.

The first officer answered for Jen. 'Sure, come on.' He started into the galley, and they rose and followed behind.

Jen passed the rest of the cocktails rapidly. A warning was tingling through her nerves, hammering at her brain. She had to get back to the galley.

The four women traveling together accepted the cocktails and gushed their thanks. At last the tray was empty. Jen dropped it flat against her side and started forward just as Allan called to her. She went to the rear of the plane where he was working at the small panel that served as a desk. 'Jen, I can't find the extra baggage decs. They're not in the briefcase anywhere.'

Jen set down the tray and bent over the briefcase. 'They were in this compartment when we were coming down this morning.' She glanced up ahead frantically, knowing it was no use trying to leave Allan until the declarations were found. The honeymooners had returned and the first officer was starting back toward the flight deck with the other young couple. Next time up, he'd be taking the three single men. Impatiently Jen shook all the papers out of the briefcase and spent agonizing minutes going through them. The declarations weren't there. She started to jam the papers back in the briefcase, but was stopped by Allan's sharp 'Cut it out, Jen. Put those papers back straight. I'm fouled up as it is.'

By the time she had the briefcase filled, the first officer was escorting the second young couple back to their seats. She watched, holding her breath, as he invited the three latecomers up forward together.

She glanced at Allan's sulky face and did not dare leave him. He met her look. 'Try my topcoat, will you? Maybe I stuck them in my pocket.'

Jen hurried to the closet, fished for Allan's coat, found it, and raced through the pockets. In the inside one, she found the missing declarations. She dropped them on his lap. 'Here they are.'

'That's a relief. Just read off the list of passengers to me and I'll see if I have all the declarations. Then we can start dinner.'

Wanting to strangle him, Jen went down the names. When she had finally finished, the group of four women were returning from the flight deck. Every passenger in the plane had gone through the galley now.

As Jen raced up the aisle, she was stopped by one of the women. 'Isn't it a little careless, Miss, to leave all those doors open in the galley? I ruined my stockings on the refrigerator handle.'

Jen stared at her, hurried forward to the galley, and slammed the door between it and the cabin. The galley was a mess. Every cabinet door was open, groceries had tumbled into the sink – and the pocketbook she had left in the refrigerator was lying open on the countertop! She didn't need to look in it to know that the magazine with the lists was gone.

She stumbled to the counter, feeling sick, and ran her fingers numbly over her purse, trying to think. Someone had managed a hurried search of the galley and had found her pocket book in the refrigerator. Whoever had done it knew she would be aware the papers were missing and would be doubly careful not to draw suspicion on himself.

Mechanically, she began to straighten up the galley, then reached for the manifest in her pocket. It had to be one of the three latecomers, Walter Hastings, Andrew Clinton or August Carlson. Maybe Bill, the first officer, had noticed if any of them didn't follow him through to the flight deck.

The flight was getting rougher. Jen steadied herself against the navigator's table as she went forward. Bill was just leaving his seat in the cockpit. He smiled at her and said, 'It was hardly worth dragging those people up for the minute they stood here. The captain got word we're heading into rough weather, so he told me to get them in and out fast. I think I overdid it, though. The last time, I left the men up here and started back to get the four women. We all met in the galley and, believe me, we didn't fit.'

Jen turned away without speaking. If Bill had left the men alone, it was useless to question him about who might have dropped back. She would have to depend on herself to find the thief and she had little time to do it. The plane tipped and she steadied herself against the door. She closed her eyes and Dick's face came into her mind – and, in sharper focus, his look when he gave her the magazine: 'Remember that carrier that vanished at the end of the Korean War?'

Jen choked back a sob. Dick, she thought, you put your life in danger for those papers. You trusted me with them, and less than an hour after you gave them to me I've lost them. There wouldn't be any headlines for the families of those boys to pore over tomorrow morning and end forever their doubt and despair. She had taken care of that. But she *couldn't* let them down – not Dick, not all those people, not all those boys whose flight, if positively known, might be solved somehow. She had to recover the lists and she had two hours to do it in.

Impatiently, she rubbed the tears from her eyes. Hastings, Clinton, Carlson – she tried to reconstruct her impressions of each man when she had served them cocktails.

Hastings in seat six – tall, thinnish, grey hair, moustache, eye-glasses, about fifty-three. He'd been deep in the financial section of *The Times* and hadn't heard her when she offered the drink. Then he'd laughed and apologized. 'Whenever I squeeze in a vacation, I never look at a paper, but the minute I start home I have to begin catching up.' Jen recalled her impression that he was the executive type completely at home on a plane.

Clinton had had a Manhattan. He had thanked her for it and sipped it quickly, saying, 'I can use this. I just got word my father had a heart attack last night.' The scion of the family, Jen decided. Very good-looking in a tanned, blond way, handsomely dressed in a light-weight blue suit and an expensive-looking tie. He looked young, about twenty-five, like an Ivy League graduate who had a station wagon and a Jaguar side by side in his garage.

Carlson, a dark, stocky man about forty-two, seemed ill at ease on the plane and shyly explained he'd been visiting his son who worked in one of the Bermuda hotels.

Jen dug her nails into her fists, thinking they all seemed so right, so typical of what they claimed to be – the businessman, the well-to-do son, the grocery clerk. But one of them was lying – which one?

The cabin door opened and she stepped aside to make room for Allan. He was looking much happier now that the paperwork was finished. 'Jen, suppose you work the galley this time and I'll serve the dinners. If you're really serious about that reporter, you might as well get some experience tossing meals together. There's no trick to carrying trays.'

Jen debated swiftly. She *had* to serve the dinners. If she spent the next hour or more in the galley, she'd never get a chance to find out who had the magazine. She searched for a plausible excuse to give Allan and could find nothing better than a headache. She rubbed her forehead. 'Allan, would you mind awfully taking over the galley? My head is splitting. I'll make it up to you next time we have a flight together.'

Allan looked concerned. 'Sure, kid. It doesn't matter to *me*. You don't look so hot at that. If you want to lie down in the bunk for a while, I can handle the meal.'

'Oh, no – no. I just can't handle the galley. But it's sweet of you to suggest it.'

Allan patted her shoulder. 'I'm a very accommodating fellow. But, then, I've always had a weakness for brunettes. You know, Jen, newspaper reporters are very undependable fellows. They haven't got half as much to offer as pursers. Or is this speech too late?'

Jen smiled. 'It's too late, for one thing, and you don't mean it, for another.'

Allan put on his rueful look and Jen knew what was coming. Allan fancied himself as a connoisseur of women and a sought-after man about town. She had to get away.

The flight-deck door into the galley opened, saving her. Bill handed in the flight chart. 'Here you are, kids. Show the folks where we are.'

Jen grabbed it from him. 'I'll bring it around.' She darted into the cabin before Allan could stop her. She started with the honeymooners, making the conventional speech. 'Perhaps you'd like to see the flight chart. This shows our course, the speed we're flying at, our altitude, the rate of the tailwinds. The X on the chart indicates our present position.'

She could have asked them to pass it back to the other passengers when they glanced at it, but instead she waited, every nerve trembling, eager for the moment she would bring it to the three men.

Handing it to Walter Hastings, the middle-aged executive, she studied him anxiously as he looked it over. The only piece of luggage he had brought into the cabin was a briefcase, now lying unzipped at his feet. Some papers from it were on his lap. The magazine with the lists might very well be in the briefcase, but if they were would he be caring enough to have the bag open? Or if he were guilty, was he playing the busy banker plunging back into work? He handed her back the chart with a murmured thank you.

She moved on to Andrew Clinton. He shook his head when she tried to hand him the chart. 'No, thanks. I'll take your word for it.' He lit a cigarette and offered her one. She refused and he nodded. 'That's right. You girls aren't supposed to smoke on duty, are you?' His eyes were blue with little brown spots near the pupil. He *was* attractive, Jen decided, liking the smart cut of his suit, the well creased trousers that had survived the hot Bermuda afternoon, his immaculate white shoes. Once she'd chided Dick about a rumpled suit he was wearing and he'd told her he thought it gave him a boyish appeal.

Jen snapped back to reality. She had to probe this young man somehow, try to get a feeling about him. She remembered his father was supposed to be ill with a heart attack. 'You must be terribly concerned about your father.'

He nodded. 'I keep thinking if I'd paid a little more attention to the business, *he'd* have taken the vacation instead and this wouldn't have happened. But I shouldn't bore you with my troubles.'

'You're not boring me at all,' Jen replied. 'But try not to worry so much. It probably isn't half as bad as the telegram sounded.'

She continued down the plane. Another blank, she thought. The solicitous son blaming himself for taking a vacation while his father works himself to death. She glanced back, noticing a small zipper bag, the kind the airline passed out to passengers, in the overhead rack at Andrew Clinton's seat. She wondered – if he had the magazine, would he dare put the bag on the rack? She shook her head in despair. He and Hastings both seemed so on the level. Maybe Carlson –

She was before him, offering the flight chart. He was a swarthy man, with a heavy-looking suit and brightly shined shoes. He looked bewildered at the chart, but when she explained he reached for it eagerly. 'My son knows all about these things. He works in the Princess Hotel. He's going to be headwaiter there someday.' He placed the flight chart on his knees, reached into his pocket, awkwardly drew out an ancient wallet, and produced a picture of a younger edition of himself. 'That's how he looks in his uniform.'

Jen glanced at the picture. 'He looks just like you.'

Pride made the little man sit straighter. 'That's what everybody says. You know, he sent me the money for this trip. He wrote me a letter' – the letter was produced – '"Papa, close up the store and come down for two weeks. This place is Paradise." '

The letter and picture were put away. The flight chart was back in Jen's hand.

Another apparent blank. This passenger had an ancient-looking black bag that stuck out from under his seat. Maybe the lists were concealed there and his uncomfortably proud air was an act – but, more likely, Jen thought, the bag contained inexpensive souvenirs for his friends back home.

She quickly finished passing the chart to the other passengers, then went to the water tank and drew a glass of water. Time was going by. Every turn of the propellers was bringing the plane nearer to New York and she still had no suspicion which of the three men had stolen the magazine. Dick's face haunted her. And all those nameless people whose boys had been on that carrier seemed to be standing around her accusingly.

She wanted to shout, Please, God, help me! She gulped down the water and looked forward. Allan had opened the top half of the galley door, making a serving table of the bottom half for the dinner trays.

Jen went back to the lounge, combed her hair, brightened her lipstick, and washed her hands. She stared in disgust at the smear on her sleeve that the salad in the refrigerator had caused. Then her expression changed from annoyance to fascination, to excitement. She remembered that she'd been very careful to keep her arm well above the salad when she hid the purse – and yet she'd still stained her sleeve. Whoever had searched for her purse had only an instant to

38

pull it out and grab the papers. Whoever had done that hadn't time to be careful and might very well have stained his sleeve, too! It was a slim chance, a pitiful hope, but it was the first tangible clue that had been offered her.

Hastings, the banker, had taken his jacket off and folded it under the papers he'd scattered about him. Had there been a reason for that?

Andrew Clinton had offered her a cigarette, with his left hand on the armrest. Was it because he was aware of a stained sleeve that would have been out of place in his trimly elegant appearance?

Carlson had dropped the flight chart on his lap when he dug for his wallet. Wouldn't it have been more natural just to hold it in his hand and reach for the wallet with his other hand?

Jen hurried out of the lounge, clicking the door shut behind her decisively. One way or another, she had to see the bottom part of the jacket sleeves of all three men.

A steaming tray was perched on the bottom part of the galley door. Allan was ready with dinner. She raced up the aisle and grabbed the tray. Allan's bantering humor was gone. He looked up from the oven where he was pulling out sizzling dinners and snapped in a low voice, 'For heaven's sake, what's eating you this trip? You know this stuff turns to mush if it gets cold, but you vanish just when I'm ready with dinner.'

Jen quickly started passing the trays. When she came to Hastings, the papers were no longer in sight, his briefcase was closed at his seat, and he was wearing his jacket. He reached up both hands for the tray and there was no trace of a stain on either sleeve. He was the well bred executive who'd tidied up for dinner.

Jen was flustered. If her hunch was correct, she could eliminate Hastings from her list of suspects.

39

Andrew Clinton was next. But when she offered him the tray, he shook his head. 'No, thanks,' he said. 'I couldn't eat a thing.' Helplessly, Jen passed the tray to one of the four women, who said, 'This looks simply delicious!'

It was Carlson's turn. He reached for his tray with his right hand. Jen could see the underneath part of that sleeve and it was unblemished. She started to turn away, then said, 'Oh, dear, I think your coffee spattered. I hope you didn't stain your sleeve.' Reaching down, she pulled his left hand up and examined his sleeve closely. Another blank.

Going forward to the galley, Jen served trays to the crew. If her hunch was right, it had to be Andrew Clinton, Jr., the would-be solicitous son, who'd stolen the papers. She finished with the crew and prepared a small tray with two steaming cups of coffee, a small sugar bowl, and a cream pitcher.

Clinton was staring out of the window and turned, startled, when she dropped down beside him. She made her eyes innocent. 'I know coffee will make you feel better,' she smiled. 'And maybe talking to someone will take your mind off things. If you don't object, I'll have my coffee with you.'

There was nothing he could do but accept her offer. She noticed that he carefully reached for the coffee with his left hand, sliding his right hand into his lap and refusing cream and sugar. Either he likes it black, she reasoned, or he doesn't want to raise his other hand to get the cream.

She began chattering to him aimlessly. She loved London – had he ever been there? Night flying was always exciting somehow. Then she broke off. 'Isn't that a perfectly gorgeous cloud bank?' He looked up as she pointed with the hand that held her coffee. Deliberately, she tilted her cup so that few drops spilled on his right hand. With a curse, he pulled his hand out of the way, then dropped it on his knee again – but not before Jen had seen the stain on the underneath part of his right sleeve.

I can't let him know that I know. The thought flashed through Jen's mind, warning her that he'd destroy the papers rather than risk carrying them if he was sure she'd traced them to him. She ignored his sleeve, pulled out her handkerchief, and gently patted his hand.

'I'm so terribly sorry.' It wasn't hard to stammer the words, make her voice breathless. She glanced at his face. His eyes were angry, calculating, but as she continued apoligizing they relaxed and became disarming.

'It's really nothing,' he said. 'Please don't be so upset.'

'You're awfully nice,' she said. 'I'm all thumbs. Don't hold it against the airline, please.'

She started collecting the empty dinner trays on her way forward. The relief at having located the person carrying the papers drained away as she realized the worst was still facing her – how to get them back. The magazine had to be in the small airline's bag in the rack over Clinton's seat.

Mechanically, she dumped the trays in the galley and came back for more. If Clinton was sure of himself, she might be able to catch him off guard. But how? If Dick were here, he'd know what to do.

Dick – just the thought of his name brought comfort, joy. 'In a few days I'll make the conventional speech,' he'd said. Would he make that speech if she failed him when he needed her so badly?

She brought the last trays up to the galley. Allan had finished tidying up, was tossing the garbage into refuse bags. 'Hey, Jen,' he inquired, giving a final wipe to the gleaming counters, 'Did you do any shopping at the Field? I've got to get the declaration ready for Customs.'

'Customs!' Jen clutched at the word. Was there any way she could recover the magazine in Customs? It was the only place Clinton would have to open his bag. How could she work it so he'd be tied up there? She remembered the ring Dick gave her. He must have forgotten that she'd have to declare it. She didn't want Allan to know she had an engagement ring – he'd be sure to tell the crew and she couldn't be bothered with that now.

'I did pick up something,' she told him. 'Leave me a declaration, will you?'

'Sure thing.' Allan pulled one out of his pocket. 'But how you can do any shopping two days before payday, I'll never know.'

Jen went back to the cabin, sat in the crew seat, and started to fill out the declaration.

'One diamond ring, value – ' She stopped, her pen poised. She didn't know what the ring was worth. She had no sales slip for it. She'd probably be in a mess trying to explain it.

An idea began in her mind and made her slowly put the pen away and rip up the declaration. It was a far-fetched chance, a desperate chance, the only chance. She went back to the clothes closet and found a light trenchcoat marked '9'. Andrew Clinton's coat. Slowly, she slipped it off the rack.

The buzzer sounded just as she finished. A drink of water for one of the ladies, then another. Allan came back from the galley. 'Five minutes to go, Jen. Better start passing out the coats.'

She passed them out in a daze, trying to flash her mind ahead. Her timing had to be exact. One hint to

Clinton and she'd be sunk. Again she longed fiercely for Dick's presence. He'd be able to handle this so much better. 'Jen, darling.' If she failed him, would he ever say that again?

She gave the short boxy coats to the women, a light covert cloth to Hastings, the tan trenchcoat to Andrew Clinton. She stood over him, quickly dropping the coat, folded, on the empty seat beside him. The bag, she noticed, was securely under his arm.

She said, 'How's your hand, Mr. Clinton? Does it hurt?'

'Not at all. And you've been very kind. I'm beginning to feel my father will be all right.'

'I'm glad. Uncertainty is awful, isn't it?' She bit her lip, knowing her words had double meaning.

The seatbelt sign was flashing. Far below, the lights of New York gleamed brilliantly, their outline familiar and welcoming. Jen turned on the mike.

'Please fasten your seatbelts for the landing and extinguish your cigarettes. We've enjoyed having you aboard. We hope you've had a pleasant flight and we'd love to see you soon again.'

She slid into the last seat, Allan beside her. Ten minutes more and she'd have some idea whether the families of those boys would have news about their sons in the morning.

Allan nudged her. 'Let's go kid. And may I say this is the damndest trip I've flown with you? You've been in a fog all afternoon.'

He opened the outside door and the sharp April wind blew in, making a memory of the warm Bermuda sun. Jen led the passengers down the ramp and across the field.

The Customs room was bright, bare-looking, and empty except for the tired, bored men behind the desk. They barely glanced at the crew's bags and waved them on. Jen stood back after she handed in a blank declaration, making a production of putting on her coat and hat, delaying her exit.

Hastings was the first passenger to clear. The Customs man opened his bag, patted the clothes in it, and snapped it shut.

Andrew Clinton was next. He gave a side glance to Jen and smiled at the Customs official. 'I've only got a change of underwear and my shaving kit. I've been called home because of illness. My bags will follow later.'

The inspector unzipped his bag and pulled out the contents. A shaving kit fell onto the counter, followed by the magazine. Jen stared at the magazine. Clinton casually reached his hand to cover it. She had to make her move now.

'Why don't you tell them about the diamond ring in the lining of your overcoat, Mr. Clinton?' she inquired.

He whirled at her, his face beet-red. 'What diamond ring?'

The Customs inspector didn't look bored any more. His eyes pierced Clinton, then sought Jen. She looked at him squarely. 'I loaned Mr. Clinton that magazine,' she explained. 'He didn't care about any we had on the plane. When I went to get it, I noticed him studying a diamond ring. I knew he hadn't declared it and I saw him slit a hole in the pocket of his raincoat with his razor and slip the ring into the lining.'

Clinton had raised his hand from the magazine. Jen snatched it as the Customs men restrained him. She turned and fled as she heard one of them say to him, 'Look, buddy, don't take it out on the girl – you should know better than to try and beat the duty.'

The elevator in the Globe building stopped at the fifth

floor. Jen stepped out and was grabbed by the shoulders. A man with iron-grey hair and a ruddy, worry-ridden face was staring at her. 'Have you got the list?'

She nodded faintly. He dropped his hands and reached for the magazine as she held it out. 'Thank God. Dick's on the phone from Bermuda. He's been holding the line open for the last half hour, worried sick. He says you were definitely followed. Did you have any trouble?'

'Is Dick still on the phone?' Jen asked.

The man pointed to a telephone with the receiver lying on the desk. 'Over there.' He himself raced to an office boy. 'Tell Charlie to reset the first two pages!'

Jen picked up the open receiver weakly, whispering Dick's name. From far away she could hear his answer. 'Jen, darling, I've never been so scared in my life. Are you all right?'

'It was pretty bad, but everything's all right, Dick. I gave the lists to your editor.'

A thousand miles away she could hear his drawn-out sigh. 'Darling,' he said, 'put on the ring right now. There isn't going to be any conventional speech. I'm not giving you a chance to give it back.'

The ring – blue-white prisms of light. Jen felt hot tears on her cheeks. 'Dick, I've lost the ring. It was the only way. It was that or the lists.'

She felt the phone being taken from her. The editor was speaking into it.

'Hop the next plane back, Dick. We'll all go shopping for a new one.'

Beauty Contest at Buckingham Palace

Sir Winston sat patiently on the sun deck of his Riviera villa and waited for the deferential reporter across the table to begin asking questions concerning his just-published sixth volume of memoirs which encompassed the last forty years of the twentieth century.

He felt slightly chilled and gave a twist to the knob on his chair, causing the sun's rays to turn more strongly in his direction. 'They got the idea for this from something called an electric blanket,' he told the reporter. 'But, bosh, you probably don't even remember that.' He bit into his cigar, reflecting that when you got to be 146 yeas old, you had to remember not to refer to events or objects that belonged in the past of more than two generations ago. Otherwise people thought you were getting fey.

'Sir Winston,' the reporter said, holding up his pencil, 'I've read every volume of yours, with the exception of this new one. Now, looking back over your long, full life, what do you consider your moment of greatest trial? When do you feel your forces of leadership and cunning were most called to the fore? Was it during England's finest hours in World War Two? Or perhaps when you arbitrated the squabble between

Russia and the United States over who got stuck with the dark side of the moon? Or – '

Sir Winston raised his hand slowly. 'My son, none of these terrible times caused my blood to run cold as did the night in 1961 when the most exalted beauty contest of the twentieth century took place.'

He took a sip of brandy, shuddering at the memory. 'It was during the early years of the reign of Elizabeth the Second,' he said. 'Jacqueline Kennedy of the United States was in the White House – as first lady, of course, not President. The first woman President wasn't elected for nearly a quarter of a century after that. Fabiola of Belgium was a recent bride. Princess Grace of Monaco was renowned for her loveliness. Sirikit of Thailand and Farah of Iran – well, someone suggested that nations meet on the basis of beauty, and out of all that a beauty contest was developed among the aforementioned ladies. The judges were Khrushchev of Russia, Nehru of India and De Gaulle of France. I knew in my bones it would a bit of a sticky wicket, but no one would believe me; and since these ladies were to be accompanied by their husbands, it seemed a good way to have an informal summit conference in the bargain.'

He reached for the brandy glass. 'So a first-prize medal was struck – a map of the world in miniature with precious stones outlining the borders of the countries – valued at a million pounds, it was. I was the master of ceremonies and the London *Times* dubbed me "Sir Bert Parks" – why, I never found out. Someone had adapted a rather ghastly song, *There She Is, Miss Head of State*, to be sung to the winner. After months of preparation, all was in readiness. The ballroom at Buckingham Palace was prepared. Invitations were issued to the *crème de la crème*, and the contestants flew over in their jets. You probably don't remember about jets either.'

Sir Winston leaned back in his chair and closed his eyes. 'It's as though it were yesterday,' he said.

The reporter waited deferentially. He knew all about the beauty contest, of course. He'd read volumes on it. Who hadn't? It was known as Sir Winston's masterpiece.

The contestants stood in the wings, ready to walk through the crowded ballroom. The assembled ladies were dressed in high-fashion evening gowns and tiaras. For the men, white tie was *de rigueur*. Flowers filled the great hall. When Sir Winston announced the first contestant, the orchestra stuck up the opening notes of *Pomp and Circumstance*. The audience didn't applaud. It bowed.

Sweeping across the room, her apricot satin gown gleaming, a million dollars' worth of jewelry sparkling on her white throat, her slim hands and her chestnut hair, was Her Majesty Elizabeth the Second, by the Grace of God, of the United Kingdom of Great Britain and Northern Ireland and of her other realms and territories, Queen, Head of the Commonwealth, Defender of the Faith. She smiled dazzlingly at the assemblage, lifted her hand in her familiar gesture of greeting and took her place on the dais.

It was the first time she'd ever been involved in a beauty contest, and although she hid her nervousness behind royal aplomb, she wondered if she'd be able to add one more title to her already impressive string – 'most beautiful first lady in the world.' Of course, she was up against such striking girls as Grace of Monaco, Jackie of the Colonies, Sirikit of Thailand, Farah of Iran and Fabiola of Belgium, but still, she'd come a long way from the tremulous bride who'd wiggled her over-ample self into the love-in-the-mist-blue going-away suit that had been Norman Hartnell's creation. Dear

Norman. He must have been a bit balmy to suggest that color. Really, she hadn't looked like the heiress to the empire at all. She'd look like the empire.

She shot a quick look over to the first row where the most important dignitaries were sitting. Philip was smiling. He had a satisfied look in his eye, so she must be looking her best. She'd almost forgiven him for that day, shortly after Charles was born, when he'd looked at her quizzically and said, 'Dear, you and your mummy will be able to swap clothes soon.' Of course, she'd got back at him. The day some months later when he commented on her vanishing waist, she'd said, 'The better to match your hairline, ducks.' He hadn't minded, though. Really, it was nice to feel his pride in her.

'You're a ripping good queen, pet, probably because you enjoy it so.' Well, it *was* her cup of tea, no two ways about it.

The flutter of admiration subsided, and the audience waited breathless for the next contestant. The English in the assemblage considered the contest over already, of course. Elizabeth had outdone even herself. It wasn't just those incredibly blue eyes, the perfect complexion, the shining hair. The girl had presence – radiance, don't you know. Shows what happens when you're born to be queen.

Sir Winston consulted the program in his hands before announcing the next contestant. Not that he needed to. Gads, that had been a harangue, trying to decide in what order they'd enter. Thank heavens, Attlee had come up with the suggestion that Elizabeth as hostess come first and the others follow in the order of the length of their reign. No delicate age problem there, and it put *the* Queen at the head, which was as it should be. Trust a lamb like Attlee to turn into a dove of peace.

'Her Majesty, Queen Sirikit of Thailand,' he announced, managing to recapture some of the sonorous goldness of his wartime voice.

There was a gasp of admiration as slender Sirikit entered. She'd worn a multicolored brocade with a suggestion of the Oriental culture of her country. It had straight lines and a slit in the front, revealing an ankle that would have been as at home on a chorus girl as on a queen. Her jet-black hair was piled high and soft on her head. Her even white teeth flashed as she smiled courteously to the gathering. She walked slowly across the room and up the dais, taking care to stand not too near Elizabeth.

If she could only win, she thought. These Westerners with their appalling ideas about Thailand – it was all the work of the book, *Anna and the King of Siam*. She'd actually heard someone at the airport remark, 'With a queen like that, do you think the King keeps a harem too?' Harem indeed! Her dear Phumiphon. Anyone knew that if he ever fell for another girl it would be because she played a mean sax or blew a French horn the most.

But all in all, this had been her year – on the best-dressed-woman's list and now, if she won this contest people would certainly take Thailand seriously. And not just for that damned silver jewelry that Phumpy was always asking her to wear to drum up trade.

There was excited comment among those who dared to whisper. What an impossible comparison, they were saying. Like choosing between Snow White and Rose Red. It wasn't a degree of beauty at all – it was a type. God pity the judges if the others looked half this well. Solomon himself would have been stumped today. You couldn't open windows and have bees sniff around in this kind of contest.

'Her Serene Highness, Princess Grace of Monaco.'

Sir Winston adjusted his spectacles. This was the one who worried him the most. His own queen could win hands down over the other contestants, he was sure, but these actresses had to be watched. He chuckled to himself. There'd been an actress in his past, half a century ago. Dear, dear Ethel. Smashing she'd been in *Captain Jinks of the Horse Marines*. And they had a way of being regal of bearing almost beyond the ones who'd been born to the bit. He bent his head forward to get a glimpse as Princess Grace swept by. Worse than he'd expected – the girl was stunning!

She remembered not to hold her head higher than Elizabeth had done. People were always watching for that sort of thing. She was glad she'd settled on the white gown. She and Rainier had hemmed and hawed half the night before they'd decided against the blue. 'You shall be the snow queen,' Rainier had decreed. 'Besides, the white gown will show up better on the new stamp issue.'

'Oh, not another stamp issue, dear,' she'd protested. 'Don't you think we're beginning to have rather more stamps than letters to put them on? We still have so many left from the last issue that we had to store them in the banquet hall. Cook put her foot down on using any more of the canisters, and the basement is already heaped.'

Rainier had looked crestfallen, then said hopefully, 'We'll have a National Letter-Writing Week again. Last time we did that, we used up the whole atticful.'

She began to ascend the dais, thinking how nice it would be to win for his sake. He did so want their country to be considered important. Those remarks that compared Monaco to Central Park certainly bugged him. And he did so much for her. Like when she'd arrived for the wedding, and he'd told her that he'd had every leak in the palace repaired in her

51

honor. It's a plumber's delight now,' he'd said proudly.

And then he'd shown her his magnificent cactus garden. 'Whenever you feel like acting, we can come out here and do a scene from *High Noon*,' he'd suggested.

The last strains of *Pomp and Circumstance* died away as she took her place on the dais. *I just love that song,* she thought. *If it weren't for those* True Love *royalty checks, it would be my favorite, hands down.* She had to catch herself from humming the last line of *True Love* as she glanced quickly around. The other girls looked just great. She gazed at the first row of dignitaries and saw that Rainier was smiling from ear to ear and fairly bursting with pride. She relaxed inside. *I hope mamma remembers to send me tomorrow's Philadelphia papers,* she thought.

Farah Diba stood impatiently in the wings. She knew her eyes were sparkling and she deliberately lowered them and willed the lines of her face into the soft Mona Lisa smile that she knew people expected of her. She was wearing a pale green gown embroidered with hundreds of tiny diamonds. Her dear lord had personally placed the new tiara, valued at a king's ransom, on her head. He'd stepped back to look at her and nodded. 'Unless those judges are fools, you'll have another title tonight, little one,' he said.

She'd smiled back at him. 'Have them beheaded if they go against me,' she suggested.

He'd looked startled. 'My ancestors could have done that, of course,' he agreed. 'It might not be considered good sportsmanship today.' He'd linked her arm in his when they started down to the ballroom.

And the funny part of it, she'd thought, *is that you still don't know you adore me. Some little part of you believes that yesterday is with you yet.*

She remembered how she and a friend were at the Sorbonne when they'd read the Shah's heartbroken message announcing his divorce from his beloved Soraya. Her friend was the sentimental kind. She'd sighed. 'No matter whom he marries, he'll always weep for Soraya.'

Farah remembered her answer. 'Weeping willows are easily transplanted.' She still believed it. Oh, granted it hadn't been easy at first. But Reza Jr had tipped the scales in her favor. And she was six years younger than Soraya. That helped too.

'Her Imperial Majesty, Farah Diba, Queen of Iran.' She heard the opening bars of the music, started out into the great ballroom and felt unutterably sure of herself. One more thing – when she won this contest, she was fast going to see that Avenue Soraya got a new name. Oh, she wouldn't think of letting them change it till now. Better to be magnanimous, but enough was enough.

She knew the assemblage was comparing her with her predecessor. But Soraya had had a beautiful predecessor too and who mentioned her now? She strode confidently up the dais. Reza was leaning forward in his seat, smiling triumphantly. She wanted to blow him a kiss. It was the outrageous sort of thing that seemed to fascinate him, but she satisfied herself with the barest hint of a wink.

And the funny part of it all, she mused, *if it weren't for the heir to the peacock throne bit, I'd have preferred a girl.*

Sir Winston cleared his throat. He hoped the sweet young girl who'd just come through hadn't heard the whispers that compared her with her predecessors. *These Near East countries*, he thought impatiently. What in deuce was wrong with having a woman succeed to the throne? Judging from some of the kings he'd known, the queens did rather a better job of it. Speaking of queens – He realized that the assemblage was

53

looking at him expectantly. Oh, yes, the new little one, Fabiola of Belgium. A sweet girl really, no match for Elizabeth – but then, who was? 'Her Majesty, Queen Fabiola of the Belgians.'

Fabiola drew in her breath sharply – but with excitement, not nervousness. She came forward in pale, shimmering pink satin, yards and yards of it, twisted and shaped into an exquisite ball gown – but no train. Dear heavens, every time she thought of that twenty-foot train she'd been married in! She'd had a stiff neck half her honeymoon from the way it pulled her back.

She walked slowly across the room, bowing slightly in response to the curtsies and cheers. She'd suggested having a comb or two in her hair and carrying a fan just to jazz her outfit with a bit of Spanish elegance. But Baudouin had looked pained. 'You can wear your mantilla and combs at a costume ball some-time,' he'd suggested.

She didn't pretend that she had the outstanding good looks of Grace or Jackie. *But I've got the Cinderella ingredient*, she thought. *I capture the imagination – spinster aunt of thirty-one nephews and nieces walks off with the biggest catch in Europe.* She smiled at Baudouin, who was sitting straight and proud in the first row of dignitaries, and thought of the day they'd met. It had been at a cocktail party, and he was introduced as Count Something-or-other. She'd been stunned. Did anyone really believe that the world's most eligible bachelor wasn't recognizable? She was just about to curtsy when she thought of that American contestant on some quiz program who had known the names of long-forgotten groups of islands, but not of Belgium's King. He'd had a reason for forgetting it. Some perverse quirk made her decide to play the same game. She'd pretended complete ignorance of the count's true identity and now she thanked her stars she did.

He'd been so relaxed. Maybe Baudy just got shy when he was running the country. Every once in a while he'd say, 'And you really didn't know me, did you, dear?' She'd have to invite that American quiz fellow to dinner sometime. She certainly owed him a truckful of Brussels sprouts. She reached the dais and glanced around the magnificent ballroom. She felt the weight of the diamond tiara on her head and drew in her breath happily. *If this doesn't beat writing fairy tales*, she thought.

Sir Winston harrumphed loudly. Last but, by Jove, certainly not least, was the newest member of the charmed circle – that lovely Kennedy girl. Oh, these Americans – they had a way about them. Positively breath-taking! His throat cleared to his satisfaction, he waited till the expectant murmur hushed, then announced grandly, 'The First Lady of the United States, Jacqueline Bouvier Kennedy.'

Oleg has outdone himself, Jackie thought as she began an easy glide across the ballroom – pale gold satin, slim-lined, but with the suggestion of a train in the back. Of course, no one curtsied to her, but the deferential head-nodding was terribly flattering. She'd been telling Elizabeth this morning about how a Washington paper had sent her over to do sketches of the Coronation. 'I felt sorry for you that day,' she'd told the Queen. 'All that ceremony. I didn't know then that I had an inaugural in my future.'

'Well, at least you rode to it in a car,' Elizabeth retorted. 'That coach they drag out for me is really too much – sways like the proverbial reed and feels like the inside of a fridge.'

'Yes,' Jackie reminded her, 'but they stick to *God Save the Queen* when you come in. Have you by any chance heard a rendition of *Jacqueline*?'

Elizabeth nodded sympathetically. 'It will never make the Hit Parade.'

Jackie smiled to herself. The Queen was really a good sport. They were going riding together in the morning too. She was passing the row of dignitaries before ascending the dais.

The President was watching her intently and he slapped his right hand firmly on his knee, so everything must be all right. If Jack stopped waving that hand, there had to be something wrong. Like the time they were in a motorcade and, after five miles of simply crawling, she'd opened her book. The minute that had got still, she knew she was in hot water. But Chaucer was such a delight.

She walked across the dais majestically and noticed how really sweet Fabiola looked. *She's as new to this routine as I am, but she's enjoying it too*, Jackie thought. *And really, she doesn't look at all annoyed about King Baudouin's glasses.* That had been the one bad moment of this trip. Jack had talked Philip and Reza and Baudouin and Rainier and the other boys into a quick game of touch football in the palace garden. And Jack, being Jack, played to win.

Now Philip was limping, and Baudouin was peering near-sightedly through his reading glasses, and Rainier had a sprained thumb. But what did it matter? Here she was, and that was all that counted. Pa Kennedy was so excited about this contest too. He'd promised her a check for a million dollars if she won. She stood at her appointed place and smiled into Jack's eyes. *We've got it all*, she thought, *Youth and looks and the children and each other and money and the White House. But whatever will we do for an encore?*

Sir Winston surveyed the dais intently. Never, never had such youth and beauty been present. He looked suspiciously at the judges. He'd just heard from an unimpeachable source that Nikita had offered to vote for Jackie Kennedy if the United States would sell Alaska back to him. And Nehru had promised to vote for Elizabeth if England erected a statue of Ghandi opposite the one of Queen Victoria. You'd expect De Gaulle to be above that kind of hanky-panky, but he'd been said to have promised Rainier that he'd cast his vote for Grace in exchange for the proceeds from Monte Carlo – just to tide France over till Algeria got straightened out.

Sir Winston settled his face into the bulldog look that had made it famous in the 'Forties. The contest had served its purpose. Among the husbands of the contestants and the judges, they'd have a summit meeting, the like of which the world had never seen. And he'd get it started over some fine old brandy.

He strode to the dais. 'We have attempted the impossible,' he thundered. 'We have tried to choose between the rose and the lily, the orchid and the jasmine.' He looked to the judges, who were nodding vigorously and gratefully. 'We shall gather these ladies into a bouquet the like of which has never been seen. To attempt to select one from amongst them goes beyond the capabilities of the finite mind . . .'

Sir Winston opened his eyes. It had been his moment of inspiration. The reporter was still sitting there, quietly attentive. 'I thought the way you disposed of the first prize was a stroke of genius, sir,' he said respectfully.

Sir Winston chuckled. 'It was, young man,' he admitted. 'It was. I remembered the prize as I finished my speech and my eyes swept the assemblage in despair. 'Twas the grace of heaven they came to rest on Mrs. Khrushchev, who was looking quite chic in black velvet and pearls. She'd always been rather notorious for her dowdiness, you know. And after a hurried consultation with the judges, from which Nikita gracefully disqualified himself, we called it a "greatest improvement" medal and pinned it on her.'

57

Voices in the Coalbin

It was dark when they arrived. Mike steered the car off the dirt road down the long driveway and stopped in front of the cottage. The real estate agent had promised to have the heat turned up and the lights on. She obviously didn't believe in wasting electricity.

An insect-repellent bulb over the door emitted a bleak yellowish beam that trembled in the steady drizzle. The small-paned windows were barely outlined by a faint flicker of light that seeped through a partially open blind.

Mike stretched. Fourteen hours a day of driving for the past three days had cramped his long, muscular body. He brushed back his dark brown hair from his forehead wishing he'd taken time to get a haircut before they left New York. Laurie teased him when his hair started to grow. 'You look like a thirty-year-old Roman Emperor, Curlytop,' she would comment. 'All you need is a toga and a laurel wreath to complete the effect.'

She had fallen asleep about an hour ago. Her head was resting on his lap. He glanced down at her, hating to wake her up. Even though he could barely make out her profile, he knew that in sleep the tense lines vanished from around her mouth and the panic-stricken expression disappeared from her face.

Four months ago the recurring nightmare had begun, the nightmare that made her shriek, *'No, I won't go with you. I won't sing with you.'*

He'd shake her awake. 'It's all right, sweetheart. It's all right.'

Her screams would fade into terrified sobs. 'I don't know who they are but they want me, Mike. I can't see their faces but they're all huddled together beckoning to me.'

He had taken her to a psychiatrist, who put her on medication and began intensive therapy. But the nightmares continued, unabated. They had turned a gifted twenty-four-year-old singer who had just completed a run as a soloist in her first Broadway musical to a trembling wraith who could not be alone after dark.

The psychiatrist had suggested a vacation. Mike told him about the summers he'd spent at his grandmother's house on Oshbee Lake forty miles from Milwaukee. 'My grandmother died last September,' he'd explained. 'The house is up for sale. Laurie's never been there and she loves the water.'

The doctor had approved. 'But be careful of her,' he warned. 'She's severely depressed. I'm sure these nightmares are a reaction to her childhood experienees, but they're overwhelming her.'

Laurie had eagerly endorsed the chance to go away. Mike was a junior partner in his father's law firm. 'Anything that will help Laurie,' his father told him. 'Take whatever time you need.'

I remember brightness here, Mike thought as he studied the shadow-filled cottage with increasing dismay. I remember the feel of the water when I dove in, the warmth of the sun on my face, the way the breeze filled the sails and the boat skimmed across the lake.

It was the end of June but it might have been early March. According to the radio, the cold spell had been gripping Wisconsin for three days. There'd better be

59

enough coal to get the furnace going, Mike thought, or else the real estate agent will lose the listing.

He had to wake up Laurie. It would be worse to leave her alone in the car, even for a minute. 'We're here, love,' he said, his voice falsely cheerful.

Laurie stirred. He felt her stiffen, then relax as he tightened his arms around her. 'It's so dark,' she whispered.

'We'll get inside and turn some lights on.'

He remembered how the lock had always been tricky. You had to pull the door to you before the key could fit into the cylinder. There was a night-light plugged into an outlet in the small foyer. The house was not warm but neither was it the bone-chilling cold he had feared.

Quickly Mike switched on the hall light. The wallpaper with its climbing ivy pattern seemed faded and soiled. The house had been rented for the five summers his grandmother was in the nursing home. Mike remembered how clean and warm and welcoming it had been when she was living there.

Laurie's silence was ominous. His arm around her, he brought her into the living room. The overstuffed velour furniture that used to welcome his body when he settled in with a book was still in place but, like the wallpaper, seemed soiled and shabby.

Mike's forehead furrowed into a troubled frown. 'Honey, I'm sorry. Coming here was a lousy idea. Do you want to go to a motel? We passed a couple that looked pretty decent.'

Laurie smiled up at him. 'Mike, I want to stay here. I want you to share with me all those wonderful summers you spent in this place. I want to pretend your grandmother was mine. Then maybe I'll get over whatever is happening to me.'

Laurie's grandmother had raised her. A fear-ridden

neurotic, she had tried to instill in Laurie fear of the dark, fear of strangers, fear of planes and cars, fear of animals. When Laurie and Mike met two years ago, she'd shocked and amused him by reciting some of the litany of hair-raising stories that her grandmother had fed her on a daily basis.

'How did you turn out so normal, so much fun?' Mike used to ask her.

'I was damned if I'd let her turn me into a certified nut.' But the last four months had proved that Laurie had not escaped after all, that there was psychological damage that needed repairing.

Now Mike smiled down at her, loving the vivid sea-green eyes, the thick dark lashes that threw shadows on her porcelain skin, the way tendrils of chestnut hair framed her oval face.

'You're so darn pretty,' he said, 'and sure I'll tell you all about Grandma. You only knew her when she was an invalid. I'll tell you about fishing with her in a storm, about jogging around the lake and her yelling for me to keep up the pace, about finally managing to outswim her when she was sixty.'

Laurie took his face in her hands. 'Help me to be like her.'

Together they brought in their suitcases and the groceries they had purchased along the way. Mike went down to the basement. He grimaced when he glanced into the coalbin. It was fairly large, a four-feet-wide by six-feet-long plankboard enclosure situated next to the furnace and directly under the window that served as an opening for the chute from the delivery truck. Mike remembered how when he was eight he'd helped his grandmother replace some of the boards on the bin. Now they all looked rotted.

'Nights get cold even in the summer but we'll always be plenty warm, Mike,' his grandmother would say cheerily as she let him help shovel coal into the old blackened furnace.

Mike remembered the bin as always heaped with shiny black nuggets. Now it was nearly empty. There was barely enough coal for two or three days. He reached for the shovel.

The furnace was still serviceable. Its rumbling sound quickly echoed throughout the house. The ducts thumped and rattled as hot air wheezed through them.

In the kitchen Laurie had unpacked the groceries and begun to make a salad. Mike grilled a steak. They opened a bottle of Bordeaux and sat side by side at the old enamel table, their shoulders companionably touching.

They were on their way up the staircase to bed when Mike spotted the note from the real estate agent on the foyer table: 'Hope you find everything in order. Sorry about the weather. Coal delivery on Friday.'

They decided to use his grandmother's room. 'She loved that metal-frame bed,' Mike said. 'Always claimed that there wasn't a night she didn't sleep like a baby in it.'

'Let's hope it works that way for me.' Laurie sighed. There were clean sheets in the linen closet but they felt damp and clammy. The boxspring and mattress smelled musty.

'Warm me up,' Laurie whispered, shivering as they pulled the covers over them.

'My pleasure.'

They fell asleep in each other's arms. At three o'clock Laurie began to shriek, a piercing, wailing scream that filled the house. 'Go away. Go away. I won't. I won't.'

It was dawn before she stopped sobbing. 'They're getting closer,' she told Mike. 'They're getting closer.'

*

The rain persisted throughout the day. The outside thermometer registered thirty-eight degrees. They read all morning curled up on the velour couches. Mike watched as Laurie began to unwind. When she fell into a deep sleep after lunch, he went into the kitchen and called the psychiatrist.

'Her sense that they're getting closer may be a good sign,' the doctor told him. 'Possibly she's on the verge of a break-through. I'm convinced the root of these nightmares is in all the old wives' tales her grandmother told Laurie. If we can isolate exactly which one has caused this fear, we'll be able to exorcise it and all the others. Watch her carefully, but remember. She's a strong girl and she wants to get well. That's half the battle.'

When Laurie woke up, they decided to inventory the house. 'Dad said we can have anything we want,' Mike reminded her. 'A couple of the tables are antiques and that clock on the mantel is a gem.' There was a storage closet in the foyer. They began dragging its contents into the living room. Laurie, looking about eighteen in jeans and a sweater, her hair tied loosely in a chignon, became animated as she went through them. 'The local artists were pretty lousy,' she laughed, 'but the frames are great. Can't you just see them on our walls?'

Last year as a wedding present, Mike's family had bought them a loft in Greenwich Village. Until four months ago, they'd spent their spare time going to garage sales and auctions looking for bargains. Since the nightmares began, Laurie had lost interest in furnishing the apartment. Mike crossed his fingers. Maybe she *was* starting to get better.

On the top shelf buried behind patchwork quilts he discovered a Victrola. 'Oh, my God, I'd forgotten about that,' he said. 'What a find! Look. Here are a bunch of old records.'

He did not notice Laurie's sudden silence as he brushed the layers of dust from the Victrola and lifted the lid. The Edison trademark, a dog listening to a tube and the caption *His Master's Voice* was on the inside of the lid. 'It even has a needle in it,' Mike said. Quickly he placed a record on the turntable, cranked the handle, slid the starter to 'On', and watched as the disk began to revolve. Carefully he placed the arm with its thin, delicate needle in the first groove.

The record was scratched. The singers' voices were male but high-pitched, almost to the point of falsetto. The effect was out of synch, music being played too rapidly. 'I can't make out the words,' Mike said. 'Do you recognize it?'

'It's "Chinatown,"' Laurie said. 'Listen.' She began to sing with the record, her lovely soprano voice leading the chorus. *Hearts that know no other world, drifting to and fro.* Her voice broke. Gasping, she screamed, *'Turn it off, Mike. Turn it off now!'* She covered her ears with her hands and sank onto her knees, her face deathly white.

Mike yanked the needle away from the record. 'Honey, what is it?'

'I don't know. I just don't know.'

That night the nightmare took a different form. This time the approaching figures were singing 'Chinatown' and in falsetto voices demanding Laurie come sing with them.

At dawn they sat in the kitchen sipping coffee. 'Mike, it's coming back to me,' Laurie told him. 'When I was little. My grandmother had one of those Victrolas. She had that same record. I asked her where the people were who were singing. I thought they had to be hiding in the house somewhere. She took me down to the basement and pointed to the coalbin. She said the voices were coming from there. She swore to me that the people who were singing were in the coalbin.

Mike put down his coffee cup. 'Good God!'

'I never went down to the basement after that. I was afraid. Then we moved to an apartment and she gave the Victrola away. I guess that's why I forgot.' Laurie's eyes began to blaze with hope. 'Mike, maybe that old fear caught up with me for some reason. I was so exhausted by the time the show closed. Right after that the nightmares started. Mike, that record was made years and years ago. The singers are all probably dead by now. And I certainly have learned how sound is reproduced. Maybe it's going to be all right.'

'You bet it's going to be all right.' Mike stood up and reached for her hand. 'You game for something? There's a coalbin downstairs. I want you to come down with me and look at it.'

Laurie's eyes filled with panic, then she bit her lip. 'Let's go,' she said.

Mike studied Laurie's face as her eyes darted around the basement. Through her eyes he realized how dingy it was. The single light bulb dangling from the ceiling. The cinder-block walls glistening with dampness. The cement dust from the floor that clung to their bedroom slippers. The concrete steps that led to the set of metal doors that opened to the backyard. The rusty bolt that secured them looked as though it had not been opened in years.

The coalbin was adjacent to the furnace at the front end of the house. Mike felt Laurie's nails dig into his palm as they walked over to it.

'We're practically out of coal,' he told her. 'It's a good thing they're supposed to deliver today. Tell me, honey, what do you see here?'

'A bin. About ten shovelfuls of coal at best. A window. I remember when the delivery truck came how

65

they put the chute through the window and the coal roared down. I used to wonder if it hurt the singers when it fell on them.' Laurie tried to laugh. 'No visible sign of anyone in residence here. Nightmares at rest, please God.'

Hand in hand they went back upstairs. Laurie yawned. 'I'm so tired, Mike. And you, poor guy, haven't had a decent night's rest in months because of me. Why don't we just go back to bed and sleep the day away. I bet anything that I won't wake up with a dream.'

They drifted off to sleep, her hand on his chest, his arms encircling her. 'Sweet dreams, love,' he whispered.

'I promise they will be. I love you, Mike. Thank you for everything.'

The sound of coal rushing down the chute awakened Mike. He blinked. Behind the shades, light was streaming in. Automatically he glanced as his watch. Nearly three o'clock. God, he really must have been bushed. Laurie was already up. He pulled khaki slacks on, stuffed his feet into sneakers, listened for sounds from the bathroom. There were none. Laurie's robe and slippers were on the chair. She must be already dressed. With sudden unreasoning dread, Mike yanked a sweatshirt over his head.

The living room. The dining room. The kitchen. Their coffee cups were still on the table, the chairs pushed back as they left them. Mike's throat closed. The hurtling sound of the coal was lessening. *The coal.* Maybe. He took the cellar stairs two at a time. Coal dust was billowing through the basement. Shiny black nuggets of coal were heaped high in the bin. He heard the snap of the window being closed. He stared down at the footsteps on the floor. The imprints of his

66

sneakers. The side-by-side impressions left when he and Laurie had come down this morning in their slippers.

And then he saw the step-by-step imprints of Laurie's bare feet, the lovely high arched impressions of her slender, fine-boned feet. The impressions stopped at the coalbin. There was no sign of them returning to the stairs.

The bell rang, the shrill, high-pitched, insistent gonglike sound that had always annoyed him and amused his grandmother. Mike raced up the stairs. Laurie. Let it be Laurie.

The truck driver had a bill in his hand. 'Sign for the delivery, sir.'

The delivery. Mike grabbed the man's arm. 'When you started the coal down the chute, did you look into the bin?'

Puzzled faded blue eyes in a pleasant weather-beaten face looked squarely at him. 'Yeah, sure, I glanced in to make sure how much you needed. You were just about out. You didn't have enough for the day. The rain's over but it's gonna stay real cold.'

Mike tried to sound calm. 'Would you have seen if someone was in the coalbin? I mean, it's dark in the basement. Would you have noticed if a slim young woman had maybe fainted in there?' He could read the deliveryman's mind. He thinks I'm drunk or on drugs. 'God damn it,' Mike shouted. 'My wife is missing. My wife is missing.'

For days they searched for Laurie. Feverishly, Mike searched with them. He walked every inch of the heavily wooded areas around the cottage. He sat, hunched and shivering on the deck as they dragged the lake. He stood unbelieving as the newly delivered coal was shoveled from the bin and heaped onto the basement floor.

Surrounded by policemen, all of whose names and faces made no impression on him, he spoke with Laurie's doctor. In a flat, disbelieving tone he told the doctor about Laurie's fear of the voices in the coalbin. When he was finished, the police chief spoke to the doctor. When he hung up, he gripped Mike's shoulder. 'We'll keep looking.'

Four days later a diver found Laurie's body tangled in weeds in the lake. Death by drowning. She was wearing her night-gown. Bits of coal dust were still clinging to her skin and hair. The police chief tried and could not soften the stark tragedy of her death. 'That was why her footsteps stopped at the bin. She must have gotten into it and climbed out of the window. It's pretty wide, you know, and she was a slender girl. I've talked again to her doctor. She probably would have committed suicide before this if you hadn't been there for her. Terrible the way people screw up their children. Her doctor said that grandmother petrified her with crazy superstitions before the poor kid was old enough to toddle.'

'She talked to me. She was getting there.' Mike heard his protests, heard himself making arrangements for Laurie's body to be cremated.

The next morning as he was packing, the real estate agent came over, a sensibly dressed, white-haired, thin-faced woman whose brisk air did not conceal the sympathy in her eyes. 'We have a buyer for the house,' she said. 'I'll arrange to have anything you want to keep shipped.'

The clock. The antique tables. The pictures that Laurie had laughed over in their beautiful frames. Mike tried to picture going into their Greenwich Village loft alone and could not.

'How about the Victrola?' the real estate agent asked. 'It's a real treasure.'

Mike had placed it back in the storage closet. Now he took it out, seeing again Laurie's terror, hearing her begin to sing 'Chinatown', her voice blending with the falsetto voices on the old record. 'I don't know if I want it,' he said.

The real estate agent looked disapproving. 'It's a collector's item. I have to be off. Just let me know about it.'

Mike watched as her car disappeared around the winding driveway. *Laurie, I want you.* He lifted the lid of the Victrola as he had five days ago, an eon ago. He cranked the handle, found the 'Chinatown' record, placed it on the turntable, turned the switch to the 'On' position. He watched as the record picked up speed, then released the arm and placed the needle in the starting groove.

'Chinatown, my chinatown . . .'

Mike felt his body go cold, *No! No!* Unable to move, unable to breathe, he stared at the spinning record.

'. . . hearts that know no other world drifting to and fro . . .'

Over the scratchy, falsetto voices of the long-ago singers, Laurie's exquisite soprano was filling the room with its heart-stopping, plaintive beauty.

That's the Ticket

If Wilma Bean had not been in Philadelphia visiting her sister Dorothy, it never would have happened. Ernie, knowing that Wilma had watched the drawing on television, would have rushed home at midnight from his job as a security guard at the Do-Shop-Here Mall in Paramus, New Jersey, and they'd have celebrated together. *Two million dollars!* That was their share of the special Christmas lottery.

Instead, because Wilma was in Philadelphia paying a pre-Christmas visit to her sister Dorothy, Ernie stopped at the Friendly Shamrock Watering Hole for a pop or two and then topped off the evening at the Harmony Bar six blocks from his home in Elmwood Park. There, nodding happily to Lou the owner-bartender, Ernie ordered his third Seven and Seven of the evening, wrapped his plump sixty-year-old legs around the bar stool, and dreamily reflected on how he and Wilma would spend their newfound wealth.

It was then that his faded blue eyes fell upon Loretta Thistlebottom who was perched on the corner stool against the wall, a stein of beer in one hand, a Marlboro in the other. Ernie thought Loretta was a very attractive woman. Tonight her brilliant blonde hair curled on her shoulders in a pageboy, her pinkish lipstick complemented her large purple-accented green eyes, and her generous bosom rose and fell with sensuous regularity.

Ernie observed Loretta with almost impersonal admiration. It was well known that Loretta Thistlebottom's husband, Jimbo Potters, a beefy truck driver, was extremely proud of the fact that Loretta had been a dancer in her early days and was also extremely jealous of her. It was hinted he wasn't above knocking Loretta around if she got too friendly with other men.

However, since Lou the bartender was Jimbo's cousin, Jimbo didn't mind if Loretta sat around the bar the nights Jimbo was on a long-distance haul. After all it was a neighborhood hang-out. Plenty of wives came in with their husbands and as Loretta frequently commented, 'Jimbo can't expect me to watch the tube by myself or go to Tupperware parties whenever he's carting garlic buds or bananas along Route 1. As a person born in the trunk to a prominent show business family, I need people around.'

Her show business career was the subject of much of Loretta's conversation and tended to grow in importance as the years passed. That was also why even though she was really Mrs. Jimbo Potters, Loretta still referred to herself as Thistlebottom, her stage name.

Now in the murky light shed by the Tiffany-type globe over the well-scarred bar, Ernie silently admired Loretta, reflecting that even though she had to be in her mid-fifties, she had kept her figure very, very well. However, he wasn't really concerned about her. The winning lottery ticket, which he had pinned to his undershirt, was warming the area around his heart. It was like having a glowing fire there. Two million dollars. That was one hundred thousand dollars a year less taxes for twenty years. They'd be collecting well into the twenty-first century. By then they might even be able to take a cook's tour to the moon.

Ernie tried to visualize the expression on Wilma's face when she heard the good news. Wilma's sister,

71

Dorothy, didn't have a television and seldom listened to the radio so down in Philadelphia Wilma wouldn't know that now she was wealthy. The minute he'd heard the good news on the portable radio, Ernie had been tempted to rush to the phone and call Wilma but immediately decided that that wouldn't be fun. Now Ernie smiled happily, his round face creasing into a merry pancake as he visualized Wilma's homecoming tomorrow. He'd pick her up at the train station at Newark. She'd ask him how close they'd come to winning. 'Did we have two of the numbers? Three of the numbers?' He'd tell her they didn't even have one of the winning combination. Then when they got home, she'd find her stocking hung on the mantel, the way they used to do when they were first married. In those days Wilma had worn stockings and garters. Now she wore queen-sized pantyhose so she'd have to dig down to the toe for the ticket. He'd say, 'Just keep looking; wait till you see the surprise.' He could just picture the way she'd scream and throw her arms around him.

Wilma had been a darn cute young girl when they were married forty years ago. She still had a pretty face and her hair a soft white-blonde was naturally wavy. She wasn't a showgirl type like Loretta but she suited him just right. Sometimes she got a little cranky about the fact that he liked to bend the elbow with the boys now and then but for the most part, Wilma was A-okay. And boy, what a Christmas they'd have this year. Maybe he'd take her to Fred the Furrier and get her a mouton lamb or something.

Contemplating the pleasure it would be to manifest his generosity, Ernie ordered his fourth Seven and Seven. His attention was diverted by the fact that Loretta Thistlebottom was engaged in a strange ritual. Every minute or two, she laid the cigarette in her right hand in the ashtray, the stein of beer in her left hand on the bar, and vigorously scratched the palm, fingers, and back of her right hand with the long pointed fingernails of her left hand. Ernie observed that her right hand was inflamed, angry red and covered with small, mean-looking blisters.

It was getting late and people were starting to leave. The couple who had been sitting next to Ernie and at a right angle to Loretta departed. Loretta, noticing that Ernie was watching her, shrugged. 'Poison ivy,' she explained. 'Would you believe poison ivy in December? That dumb sister of Jimbo decided she had a green thumb and made her poor jerk of a husband rig up a greenhouse off their kitchen. So what does she grow? Weeds and poison ivy. That takes real talent.' Loretta shrugged and repossessed the stein of beer and her cigarette. 'So how ye been, Ernie? Anything new in your life?'

Ernie was cautious. 'Not much.'

Loretta sighed. 'Me neither. Same old stuff. Jimbo and me are saving to get out of here next year when he retires. Everyone tells me Fort Lauderdale is a real swinging place. Jimbo's getting piles from all these years driving the rig. I keep telling him how much money I could make as a waitress to help out but he don't want anyone flirting with me.' Loretta scratched her hand against the bar and shook her head. 'Can you imagine after twenty-five years, Jimbo still thinks every guy in the world wants me? I kind of love it but it can be a pain in the neck, too.' Loretta sighed, a world-weary sigh. 'Jimbo's the most passionate guy I ever knew and that's saying something. But as my mother used to say, a good roll in the sack is even better when there's a full wallet between the spring and mattress.'

'Your mother said that?' Ernie was bemused at the

73

practical wisdom. He began to sip his fourth Seagrams and Seven-Up.

Loretta nodded. 'She was a million laughs but she told it straight. The heck with it. Maybe someday I'll win the lottery.'

The temptation was too great. Ernie slipped over the two empty bar stools as fast as his out-of-shape body would permit. 'Too bad you don't have my luck,' he whispered.

As Lou the bartender yelled, 'Last call, folks,' Ernie patted his massive chest in the spot directly over his heart.

'Like they say, Loretta, "X marks the spot." There were sixteen winnin' tickets in the special Christmas drawing. One of them is right here pinned to my underwear.' Ernie realized that his tongue was beginning to feel pretty heavy. His voice sank into a furtive whisper. *'Two million dollars.* How about that?' He put his finger to his lips and winked.

Loretta dropped her cigarette and let it burn unnoticed on the long-suffering surface of the bar. *'You're kidding!'*

'I'm not kidding.' Now it was a real effort to talk. 'Wilma 'n me always bet the same number 1-9-4-7-5-2. 1947 'cause that was the year I got out of high school. 'Fifty-two, the year Wee Willie was born.' His triumphant smile left no doubt to his sincerity. 'Crazy thing is Wilma don't even know yet. She's visiting her sister Dorothy and won't get home till tomorrow.'

Fumbling for his wallet, Ernie signaled for his check. Lou came over and watched as Ernie stood uncertainly on the suddenly tilting floor. 'Ernie, wait around,' Lou ordered. 'You're bombed. I'll drive you home when I close up. You gotta leave your car here.'

Insulted, Ernie started for the door. Lou was insinuating he was tanked. What a nerve. Ernie opened the door of the woman's restroom and was in a stall before he realized his mistake.

Sliding off the bar stool, Loretta said hurriedly. 'Lou, I'll drop him off. He only lives two blocks from me.'

Lou's skinny forehead furrowed. 'Jimbo might not like it.'

'So don't tell him.' They watched as Ernie lurched unsteadily out from the woman's restroom. 'For Pete's sake, do you think he'll make a pass at me?' she asked scornfully.

Lou made a decision. 'You're doing me a favor, Loretta. *But don't tell Jimbo.*'

Loretta let out her fulsome ha-ha bellow. 'Do you think I want to risk my new caps? They won't be paid for for another year.'

From somewhere behind him Ernie vaguely heard the din of voices and laughter. Suddenly he was feeling pretty rotten. The speckled pattern of the tile floor began to dance, causing a sickening whirl of dots to revolve before his eyes. He felt someone grasp his arm. 'I'm gonna drop you off, Ernie.' Through the roaring in his ears, Ernie recognized Loretta's voice.

'Damn nice of you, Loretta,' he mumbled. 'Guess I chelebrated too much.' Vaguely he realized that Lou was saying something about having a Christmas drink on the house when he came back for his car.

In Loretta's aging Bonneville Pontiac he leaned his head back against the seat and closed his eyes. He was unaware that they had reached his driveway until he felt Loretta shaking him awake. 'Gimme your key, Ernie. I'll help you in.'

His arm around her shoulders, she steadied him along the walk. Ernie heard the scraping of the key in the lock, felt his feet moving through the living room down the brief length of the hallway.

'Which one?'

'Which one?' Ernie couldn't get his tongue to move.

'Which bedroom?' Loretta's voice sounded irritated. 'Come on, Ernie, you're no feather to drag around. Oh, forget it. It has to be the other one. This one's full of those statues of birds your daughter makes. Cripes, you couldn't give them away as a door prize in a looney bin. No one's *that* nutty.'

Ernie felt a flash of instinctive resentment at Loretta's putdown of his daughter, Wilma Jr, Wee Willie as he called her. Wee Willie had real talent. Someday she'd be a famous sculptor. She'd lived in New Mexico ever since she dropped out of school in 'sixty-eight and supported herself working evenings as a waitress at McDonald's. Days she made pottery and sculpted birds.

Ernie felt himself being turned around and pushed down. His knees buckled and he heard the familiar speak of the boxspring. Sighing in gratitude, in one simultaneous movement, he stretched out and passed out.

Wilma Bean and her sister Dorothy had had a pleasant day. In small doses Wilma enjoyed being with Dorothy who was sixty-three to Wilma's fifty-eight. The trouble was that Dorothy was very opinionated and highly critical of both Ernie and Wee Willie and Wilma could take just so much of that. But she was sorry for Dorothy. Dorothy's husband had walked out on her ten years before and now was living high on the hog with his second wife, a karate instructor. Dorothy and her daughter-in-law did not get along very well. Dorothy still worked part-time as a claims adjuster in an insurance office and as she frequently told Wilma, 'the phony claims don't get past me.'

Very few people believed they were sisters. Dorothy was, as Ernie put it, like one side of eleven, just straight up and down with thin gray hair which she wore in a tight knot at the back of her head. Ernie always said she should have been cast as Carrie Nation; she'd have looked good with a hatchet in her hand. Wilma knew that Dorothy was still jealous that Wilma had been the pretty one and that even though she'd gotten heavy, her face hadn't wrinkled or even changed very much. But still, Wilma theorized, blood is thicker than water and a weekend in Philadelphia every four months or so and particularly around holiday time was always enjoyable.

The afternoon of the lottery drawing day, Dorothy picked Wilma up from the train station. They had a late lunch at Burger King, then drove around the neighborhood where Grace Kelly had been raised. They had both been her avid fans. After mutually agreeing that Prince Albert ought to marry, that Princess Caroline had certainly calmed down and was doing a fine job, and that Princess Stephanie should be slapped into a convent until she straightened out, they went to a movie, then back to Dorothy's apartment. She had cooked a chicken and over dinner, late into the evening, they gossiped.

Dorothy complained to Wilma that her daughter-in-law had no idea how to raise a child and was too stubborn to accept even the most helpful suggestions.

'Well, at least you have grandchildren,' Wilma sighed. 'No wedding bells in sight for Wee Willie. She has her heart set on her sculpting career.'

'What sculpting career?' Dorothy snapped.

'If we could just afford a good teacher,' Wilma sighed, trying to ignore the dig.

'Ernie shouldn't encourage Willie.' Dorothy said bluntly. 'Tell him not to make such a fuss over that junk she sends home. Your place looks like a crazy man's version of a birdhouse. How is Ernie? I hope you're keeping him out of bars. Mark my words. He has the makings of an alcoholic. All those broken veins in his nose.'

Wilma thought of the outsized Christmas boxes that had arrived from Wee Willie a few days ago. Marked *Do not open till Christmas*, they'd been accompanied by a note. 'Ma, wait till you see these. I'm into peacocks and parrots.' Wilma also thought of the staff Christmas party at the Do-Shop-Here Mall the other night when Ernie had gotten schnockered and pinched the bottom of one of the waitresses.

Knowing that Dorothy was right about Ernie's ability to lap up booze did not ease Wilma's resentment at having the truth pointed out to her. 'Well, Ernie may get silly when he has a drop or two too much but you're wrong about Wee Willie. She has real talent and when my ship comes in I'll help her to prove it.'

Dorothy helped herself to another cup of tea. 'I suppose you're still wasting money on lottery tickets.'

'Sure am,' Wilma said cheerfully, fighting to retain her good nature. 'Tonight's the special Christmas drawing. If I were home I'd be in front of the set praying.'

'That combination of numbers you always pick is ridiculous! 1-9-4-7-5-2. I can understand a person using the year her child was born but the year Ernie graduated from high school? That's ridiculous.'

Wilma had never told Dorothy that it had taken Ernie six years to get through high school and his family had had a block party to celebrate. 'Best party I was ever at,' he frequently told her, memory brightening his face. 'Even the mayor came.'

Anyhow, Wilma liked that combination of numbers. She was absolutely certain that someday they

78

would win a lot of money for her and Ernie. After she said good night to Dorothy and puffing with the effort made up the sofabed where she slept on her visits, she reflected that as Dorothy grew older she got crankier. She also talked your ear off and it was no wonder her daughter-in-law referred to her as 'that miserable pain in the neck.'

The next day Wilma got off the train in Newark at noon. Ernie was picking her up. As she walked to their meeting spot at the main entrance to the terminal she was alarmed to see Ben Gump, the next-door neighbor, there instead.

She rushed to Ben, her ample body tensed with fear. 'Is anything wrong? Where's Ernie?'

Ben's wispy face broke into a reassuring smile. 'No, everything's just fine, Wilma. Ernie woke up with a touch of flu or something. Asked me to come for you. Heck, I've got nothing to do 'cept watch the grass grow.' Ben laughed heartily at the witticism that had become his trademark since his retirement.

'Flu,' Wilma scoffed. 'I'll bet.'

Ernie was a reasonably quiet man and Wilma had looked forward to a restful drive home. At breakfast, Dorothy, knowing she was losing her captive audience, had talked nonstop, a waterfall of acid comments that had made Wilma's head throb.

To distance herself from Ben's snail-paced driving and long-winded stories, Wilma concentrated on the pleasurable excitement of looking in the paper the minute she arrived home and checking the lottery results. '1-9-4-7-5-2, 1-9-4-7-5-2,' she chanted to herself. It was silly. The drawing was over but even so she had a *good* feeling. Certainly Ernie would have phoned her if they'd won but even coming close, like getting three or four of the six numbers, made her know that their luck was changing.

She spotted the fact the car wasn't in the driveway and guessed the reason. It was probably parked at the Harmony Bar. She managed to get rid of Ben Gump at the door, thanking him profusely for picking her up but ignoring his broad hints that he sure could use a cup of coffee. Then Wilma went straight to the bedroom. As she'd expected, Ernie was in bed. The covers were pulled to the tip of his nose. One look told her he had a massive hangover. 'When the cat's away the mouse will play.' She sighed. 'I hope your head feels like a balloon-sized rock.'

In her annoyance, she knocked over the four-foot-high pelican that Wee Willie had sent for Thanksgiving and that was perched on a table just outside the bedroom door. As it clattered to the floor, it took with it the pottery vase, an early work of Wee Willie's, and the arrangement of plastic baby's breath and poinsettias Wilma had labored over in preparation for Christmas.

Sweeping up the broken vase, rearranging the flowers and restoring the pelican, now missing a section of one wing, to the tabletop stretched Wilma's patience to the breaking point.

But the thought of the magic moment of looking up to see how close they'd come to winning the lottery and maybe finding that this time they'd come *really* close restored her to her usual good temper. She made a cup of coffee and fixed cinnamon toast before she settled at the kitchen table and opened the paper.

Sixteen Lucky Winners Share Thirty-Two Million Dollar Prize, the headline read.

Sixteen lucky winners. Oh to be one of them. Wilma said her hand over the winning combination. She's read the numbers one digit at a time. It was more fun that way.

'1-9-4-7-5'

Wilma sucked in her breath. Her head was pounding. Was it possible? In an agony of suspense she removed her palm from the final number.

'2'

Her shriek and the sound of the kitchen chair toppling over caused Ernie to sit bolt upright in bed. Judgment Day was at hand.

Wilma rushed into the room, her face transfixed. 'Ernie, why didn't you tell me? *Give me the ticket!*'

Ernie's head sunk down on his neck. His voice was a broken whisper. 'I lost it.'

Loretta had known it was inevitable. Even so, the sight of Wilma Bean marching up the snow-dusted cement walk followed by a reluctant, downcast Ernie did cause a moment of sheer panic. 'Forget it,' Loretta told herself. 'They don't have a leg to stand on.' She'd covered her tracks completely, she promised herself as Wilma and Ernie came up the steps to the porch between the two evergreens that Loretta had decked out with dozens of Christmas lights. She had her story straight. She had walked Ernie to the door of his home. Anyone knowing how jealous Big Jimbo was would understand that Loretta would not step beyond the threshold of another man's home when his wife wasn't present.

When Wilma asked about the ticket, Loretta would ask 'What ticket?' Ernie never *mentioned* a ticket to her. He was in no condition to talk about anything sensible. Ask Lou, Ernie was pie-eyed after a coupla drinks. He'd probably stopped somewhere else first.

Did Loretta buy a lottery ticket for the special Christmas drawing? Sure she bought some. Wanna see them? Every week when she thought of it, she'd pick up a few. Never in the same place. Maybe at the liquor store, the stationery store. You know just for luck. Always numbers she thought of off the top of her head.

Loretta scratched her right hand viciously. Damn poison ivy. She had the 1-9-4-7-5-2 winning ticket safely hidden in the sugar bowl of her best china. You had a year to claim your winnings. Just before the year was up, she'd 'accidentally' come across it. Let Wilma and Ernie try to howl that it was theirs.

The bell rang. Loretta patted her bright gold hair which she'd teased into the tossed salad look, straightened the shoulder pads of her brilliantly sequined sweater, and hurried to the closet-sized foyer. As she opened the door she willed her face to become a wreath of smiles not even minding that she was trying not to smile too much. Her face was starting to wrinkle, a genetic family problem. She constantly worried about the fact that by age sixty her mother's face had looked as though it could hold nine days of rain. 'Wilma, Ernie, what a delightful surprise,' she gushed. 'Come in. Come in.'

Loretta decided to ignore the fact that neither Wilma nor Ernie answered her, that neither bothered to brush the snow from their overshoes on the foyer mat that specifically invited guests to do that very thing, that they had no friendly holiday smiles to match her greeting.

Wilma declined the invitation to sit down, to have a cup of tea or a Bloody Mary. She made her case clear. Ernie had been holding a two-million dollar lottery ticket. He'd told Loretta about it at the Harmony Bar. Loretta had driven him home from the Harmony, gotten him into his room. Ernie had passed out and the ticket was gone.

In 1945 before she became a full-time hoofer, Loretta had studied acting at the Sonny Tufts School for Thespians. Drawing on the long-ago experience, she earnestly and sincerely performed her well-practiced scenario for Wilma and Ernie. Ernie never breathed a word to her about a winning ticket. She only drove him home as a favor to him and to Lou. Lou couldn't leave and anyhow Lou's such a runt, he couldn't fight Ernie for the car keys. 'At least you agreed to let me drive,' Loretta said to Ernie indignantly. 'I took my life in my hands just letting you snore your way home in my car.' She turned to Wilma and woman-to-woman reminded her: 'You know how jealous Jimbo is of me, silly man. You'd think I was sixteen. But no way do I go into your house unless you're there, Wilma. Ernie, you got smashed real fast at the Harmony. Just ask Lou. Did you stop anywhere else first and maybe talk to someone about the ticket?'

Loretta congratulated herself as she watched the doubt and confusion on both their faces. A few minutes later they left. 'I hope you find it. I'll say a prayer,' she promised piously. She would not shake hands with them, explaining to Wilma about her dumb sister-in-law's greenhouse harvest of poison ivy. 'Come have a Christmas drink with Jimbo and me,' she urged. 'He'll be home about four o'clock Christmas Eve.'

At home, sitting glumly over a cup of tea, Wilma said, 'She's lying. I know she's lying but who could prove it? Fifteen winners have shown up already. One missing and with a year to claim.' Frustrated tears rolled unnoticed down Wilma's cheeks. 'She'll let the whole world know she buys a ticket here, a ticket there. She'll do that for the next fifty-one weeks and then *bingo* she'll find the ticket she forgot she had.'

Ernie watched his wife in abject silence. A weeping Wilma was an infrequent sight. Now as her face blotched and her nose began to run, he handed her his red bandana handkerchief. His sudden gesture caused a ceramic hummingbird to fall off the sideboard behind him. The beak of the hummingbird crumbled against the imitation marble tile in the breakfast nook of the kitchen and brought a fresh wail of grief from Wilma.

'My big hope was that Wee Willie could give up working nights at McDonald's and study and do her birds full-time,' Wilma sobbed. 'And now that dream is busted.'

Just to be absolutely sure, they went to the Friendly Shamrock near the Do-Shop-Here Mall in Paramus. The evening bartender confirmed that Ernie had been there the night before just around midnight, had two maybe three drinks but never said boo to anybody. 'Just sat there grinning like the cat who ate the canary.'

After a dinner which neither of them touched Wilma carefully examined Ernie's undershirt which still had the safety pin in place. 'She didn't even bother to unpin it,' Wilma said bitterly. 'Just reached in and tore it off.'

'Can we sue her?' Ernie suggested tentatively. The enormity of his stupidity kept building by the minute. Getting drunk. Talking his head off to Loretta.

Too tired to even answer, Wilma opened the suitcase she had not yet unpacked and reached for her flannel nightgown. 'Sure we can sue her,' she said sarcastically, 'for having a fast brain when she's dealing with a wet brain. Now turn off the light, go to sleep, and quit that damn scratching. You're driving me crazy.'

Ernie was tearing at his chest in the area around his heart. 'Something itches,' he complained.

A bell sounded in Wilma's head as she closed her eyes. She was so worn out she fell asleep almost immediately but her dreams were filled with lottery tickets floating through the air like snowflakes. From time to time she was pulled awake by Ernie's restless movements. Usually, Ernie slept like a hibernating bear.

Christmas Eve dawned gray and cheerless. Wilma dragged herself around the house, going through the motions of putting presents under the tree. The two boxes from Wee Willie. If they hadn't lost the winning ticket they could have phoned Wee Willie to come home for Christmas. Maybe she wouldn't have come. Wee Willie didn't like the middle-class trap of the suburban environment. In that case Ernie could have thrown up his job and they could have visited her in Arizona soon. And Wilma could have bought the forty-inch television that had so awed her in Trader Horn's last week. Just think of seeing J. R. forty inches big.

Oh well. Spilt milk. No, spilt *booze*. Ernie had told her about his plans to put the lottery ticket in her pantyhose on the mantel of the fake fireplace if he hadn't lost it. Wilma tried not to dwell on the thrill of finding the ticket there.

She was not pleasant to Ernie who was still hung over and had phoned in sick for the second day. She told him exactly where he could stuff his headache.

In mid-afternoon, Ernie went into the bedroom and closed the door. After a while, Wilma became alarmed and followed him. Ernie was sitting on the edge of the bed, his shirt off, plaintively scratching his chest. 'I'm all right,' he said, his face still covered with the hangdog expression that was beginning to seem permanent. 'It's just I'm so damn itchy.'

Only slightly relieved that Ernie had not found some way to commit suicide, Wilma asked irritably, 'What are you so itchy about. It isn't time for your allergies to start. I hear enough about them all summer.'

She looked closely at the inflamed skin. 'For God's

sake, that's poison ivy. Where did you manage to pick that up?'

Poison ivy.

They stared at each other.

Wilma grabbed Ernie's undershirt from the top of the dresser. She'd left it there, the safety pin still in it, the sliver of ticket a silent, hostile witness to his stupidity. 'Put it on,' she ordered.

'But . . .'

'Put it on!'

It was instantly evident that the poison ivy was centered in the exact spot where the ticket had been hidden.

'That lying hoofer.' Wilma thrust out her jaw and straightened her shoulders. 'She said that Big Jimbo was gonna be home around four, didn't she?'

'I think so.'

'Good. Nothing like a reception committee.'

At three-thirty they pulled in front of Loretta's house and parked. As they'd expected, Jimbo's six-teen-wheel rig was not yet there. 'We'll sit here for a few minutes and make that crook nervous,' Wilma decreed.

They watched as the vertical blinds in the front window of Loretta's house began to bob erratically. At three minutes of four, Ernie pointed a nervous hand. 'There. At the light. That's Jimbo's truck.'

'Let's go,' Wilma told him.

Loretta opened the door, her face again wreathed in a smile. With grim satisfaction Wilma noticed that the smile was very, very nervous.

'Ernie. Wilma. How nice. You did come for a Christmas drink.'

'I'll have my Christmas drink later,' Wilma told her. 'And it'll be to celebrate getting our ticket back. How's your poison ivy, Loretta?'

'Oh, starting to clear up. Wilma, I don't like the tone of your voice.'

'That's a crying shame.' Wilma walked past the sectional which was upholstered in a red-and-black checkered pattern, went to the window, and pulled back the vertical blind. 'Well, what do you know? Here's Big Jimbo. Guess you two lovebirds can't wait to get your hands on each other. Guess he'll be real mad when I tell him I'm suing you for heartburn because you've been fooling around with my husband.'

'I've what?' Loretta's carefully applied purple-kisses lipstick deepened as her complexion faded to grayish white.

'You heard me. And I got proof. Ernie, take off your shirt. Show this husband-stealer your rash.'

'Rash,' Loretta moaned.

'Poison ivy just like yours. Started on his chest when you stuck your hand under his underwear to get the ticket. Go ahead. Deny it. Tell Jimbo you don't know nothing about a ticket, that you and Ernie were just having a go at a little hanky-panky.'

'You're lying. Get out of here. Ernie, don't unbutton that shirt.' Frantically Loretta grabbed Ernie's hands.

'My what a big man Jimbo is,' Wilma said admiringly as he got out of the truck. She waved to him. 'A real big man.' She turned. 'Take off your pants too, Ernie.' Wilma dropped the vertical blind and hurried over to Loretta. 'He's got the rash *down there*,' she whispered.

'Oh, my God. I'll get it. I'll get it. Keep your pants on!' Loretta rushed to the junior-sized dining room and flung open the china closet that contained the remnants of her mother's china. With shaking fingers she reached for the sugar bowl. It dropped from her hands and smashed as she grabbed the lottery ticket. Jimbo's key was turning in the door as she jammed the ticket in Wilma's hand. 'Now get out. And don't say nothing.'

Wilma sat down on the red-and-black checkered couch. 'It would look real funny to rush out. Ernie and I will join you and Big Jimbo in a Christmas drink.'

The houses on their block were decorated with Santa Clauses on the roofs, angels on the lawn, and ropes of lights framing the outside of the windows. With a peaceful smile as they arrived home, Wilma remarked how real pretty the neighborhood was. Inside the house, she handed the lottery ticket to Ernie. 'Put this in my stocking just the way you meant to.'

Meekly he went into the bedroom and selected her favorite pantyhose, the white ones with rhinestones. She fished in his drawer and came out with one of his dress-up argyle socks, somewhat lumpy because Wilma wasn't much of a knitter but still his best. As they tacked the stockings to the mantel over the artificial fireplace, Ernie said, 'Wilma, I don't have poison ivy,' his voice sunk into a faint whisper, 'down there.'

'I'm sure you don't but it did the trick. Now just put the ticket in my stocking and I'll put your present in yours.'

'You bought me a present? After all the trouble I caused? Oh, Wilma.'

'I didn't buy it. I dug it out of the medicine cabinet and put a bow on it.' Smiling happily, Wilma dropped a bottle of calamine lotion into Ernie's argyle sock.

Death on the Cape

It was the August afternoon shortly after they arrived at their rented cottage in the Village of Dennis on Cape Cod that Alvirah Meehan noticed that there was something very odd about their next-door neighbor, a painfully thin young woman who seemed to be in her late twenties.

After Alvirah and Willy looked around their cottage a bit, remarking favorably about the four-poster maple bed, the hooked rugs, the cheery kitchen and the fresh sea-scented breeze, they unpacked their expensive new clothes from their matching Vuitton luggage. Willy then poured an ice-cold beer for each to enjoy on the deck of the house that overlooked Cape Cod Bay.

Willy, his rotund body eased onto a padded wicker chaise longue, remarked that it was going to be one heck of a sunset and thank God to get a little peace. Two years before, they had won $40 million in the New York State lottery. Ever since, it seemed to Willy, Alvirah had been a walking lightning rod. First she went to the famous Cypress Point Spa in California and nearly got murdered. Then they had gone on a cruise together and – wouldn't you know – the man who sat next to them at the community table in the dining room ended up dead as a mackerel. Still, with the accumulated wisdom of his fifty-nine years, Willy was sure that in Cape Cod at least they'd have the quiet he'd been searching for. If Alvirah wrote an article for the *New York Globe* about this vacation, it would have to do with the weather and the fishing.

During his narration, Alvirah was sitting at the picnic table, a companionable few feet from Willy's stretched-out form. She wished she'd remembered to put on a sun hat. The beautician at Sassoon's had warned her against getting sun on her hair. 'It's such a lovely rust shade now, Mrs. Meehan. We don't want it to get those nasty yellow streaks, do we?'

Since recovering from the attempt on her life at the spa, Alvirah had regained all the weight she'd paid $3,000 to lose and was again a comfortable size somewhere between a fourteen and a sixteen. But Willy constantly observed that when he put his arms around her, he knew he was holding a woman – not one of those half-starved zombies you see in the fashion ads Alvirah was so fond of studying.

Forty years of affectionately listening to Willy's observations had left Alvirah with the ability to hear him with one ear and close him out with the other. Now as she gazed at the tranquil cottages perched atop the grass and sand embankment that served as a seawall, then down below at the sparkling blue-green water and the stretch of rock-strewn beach, she had the troubled feeling that maybe Willy was right. Beautiful as the Cape was, and even though it was a place she had always longed to visit, she might not find a newsworthy story here for her editor, Charles Evans.

Two years ago Charley had sent a reporter to interview the Meehans on how it felt to win $40 million. What would they do with it? Alvirah was a cleaning woman, Willy a plumber. Would they continue in their jobs?

Alvirah had told the reporter in no uncertain terms

that she wasn't that dumb. That the next time she picked up a broom it would be when she was dressed as a witch for a Knights of Columbus costume party. Then she had made a list of all the things she wanted to do, and first was the visit to Cypress Point Spa – where she planned to hobnob with the celebrities she'd been reading about all her life.

That had led Charley Evans, the editor at the *Globe*, to ask her to write an article about her stay at the spa. He gave her a sunburst pin that contained a microphone so that she could record the people she spoke with and play the tape back when she wrote the article.

The thought of her pin brought an unconscious smile to Alvirah's face.

As Willy said, she'd gotten into hot water at Cypress Point. She'd picked up on what was really going on and was nearly murdered for her trouble. But it had been so exciting and now she was great friends with everyone at the spa and could go there every year as a guest. And thanks to her help solving the murder on the ship last year, they had an invitation to have a free cruise to Alaska anytime they desired.

Cape Cod was beautiful, but Alvirah had a sneaky suspicion that this might be an ordinary vacation that wouldn't make good copy for the *Globe*.

Precisely at that moment she glanced over the row of hedges on the right perimeter of their property and observed a young woman with a somber expression standing at the railing of her porch next door and staring at the Bay.

It was the way her hands were gripping the railing: Tension, Alvirah thought. She's stuffed with it. It was the way the young woman turned her head, looked straight into Alvirah's eyes, then turned away again. She didn't even see me, Alvirah decided. The fifty- to sixty-foot distance between them did not prevent her from realizing that waves of pain and despair were radiating from the young woman.

Clearly it was time to learn what was going on. 'I think I'll just introduce myself to our neighbor,' she said to Willy. 'There's something up with her.' She walked down the steps and strolled over to the hedge. 'Hello,' she said in her friendliest voice. 'I saw you drive in. We've been here for two hours so I guess that makes us the welcoming committee. I'm Alvirah Meehan.'

The young woman turned and Alvirah felt instant compassion. She looked as though she had been ill. That ghostly pallor, the soft unused muscles of her arms and legs. 'I came here to be alone, not to be neighborly,' she said quietly. 'Excuse me, please.' That probably would have been the end of it, as Alvirah later observed, except that as she spun on her heel the girl tripped over a foot-rest and fell heavily onto the porch. Alvirah rushed to help her up, refused to allow her to go into her cottage unaided and, feeling responsible for the accident, wrapped an ice pack around her rapidly swelling wrist. By the time she had satisfied herself that the wrist was only sprained and made her a cup of tea, Alvirah had learned that her name was Cynthia Rogers and that she was a school-teacher from Illinois. That piece of information fell like a lead balloon on Alvirah's ears because, as she told Willy when she returned to their place an hour later, within ten minutes she'd recognized their neighbor. 'She might call herself Cynthia Rogers,' Alvirah confided to Willy, 'but her real name is Cynthia Lathem. She was found guilty of murdering her step-father twelve years ago. He had big bucks. I remember the case like it was yesterday.'

'You remember everything like it was yesterday,' Willy commented.

'That's the truth. And you know I always read about murders. Anyhow, this one happened here on Cape Cod. Cynthia swore she was innocent, and she always said there was a witness who could prove she'd been out of the house at the time of the murder, but the jury didn't believe her story. I wonder why she came back? I'll have to call the *Globe* and have Charley Evans send me the files on the case. She's probably just been released from prison. Her complexion is pure gray. Maybe,' and now Alvirah's eyes began to snap and sparkle, 'she's up here still looking for that missing witness to prove her story. My goodness, Willy, I just know these are going to be exciting days.'

To Willy's dismay, Alvirah opened the top drawer of the dresser, took out her sunburst pin with the hidden microphone and then began to dial her editor's direct line in New York.

That night Willy and Alvirah ate at the Red Pheasant Inn. Alvirah wore a beige and blue print dress she had bought at Bergdorf Goodman but which, as she remarked to Willy, somehow didn't look much different on her than the print dress she'd bought in Alexander's just before they won the lottery. 'It's my full figure,' she lamented as she spread butter on a warm cranberry muffin. 'My, these muffins are good. And, Willy, I'm glad that you bought the yellow linen jacket. It shows up your blue eyes, and you still have a find head of hair.'

'I feel like a two-hundred-pound canary,' Willy commented, 'but as long as you like it.'

After dinner they went to the Cape Cod Playhouse and thrilled to the performance of Debbie Reynolds in a new comedy being tried out for Broadway. At intermission, as they sipped ginger ale on the grass outside the theater, Alvirah told Willy how she'd always enjoyed Debbie Reynolds from the time Debbie was a kid doing musicals with Mickey Rooney and that it was a terrible thing Eddie Fisher ditched her when they had those two small babies. 'And what good did it do him?' Alvirah philosophized as the warning came to return to their seats for the second act. 'He never had much luck after that. People who don't do the right thing usually don't win in the end.' That comment led Alvirah to wonder whether the editor had sent the information on their neighbor by express mail. She couldn't wait to read it.

As Alvirah and Willy were enjoying Debbie Reynolds, Cynthia Lathem was at last beginning to realize that she was really free, that twelve years of prison were behind her. Twelve years ago . . . she'd been about to start her junior year at the Rhode Island School of Design when her stepfather, Stuart Richards, was found shot to death in the study of his mansion, a stately eighteenth-century captain's house in Dennis.

That afternoon Cynthia had driven past the house on her way to the cottage and pulled off the road to study it. Who was there now? she wondered. Had her stepsister Lillian sold it or had she kept it? It had been in the Richards' family for three generations, but Lillian had never been sentimental. And then Cynthia had pressed her foot on the accelerator, chilled at the rush of memories of that awful night and the days that followed. The accusation. The arrest, arraignment, trial. Her early confidence, 'I can absolutely prove that I left the house at eight o'clock and didn't get home till past midnight. I was on a date.'

Now Cynthia shivered and wrapped the light-blue woollen robe more tightly around her slender body. She'd weighed 125 pounds when she went to prison. Her present weight, 110, was not enough for her five foot eight inch height. Her hair, once a dark blonde, had changed in those years to a medium brown. Drab, she thought as she brushed it. Her eyes, the same shade of hazel as her mother's, were listless and vacant. At lunch that last day, Stuart Richards had said, 'You look more like your mother all the time, I should have had the brains to hang on to her.'

Her mother had been married to Stuart from the time Cynthia was eight until she was twelve, the longest of his two marriages. Lillian, his only natural child, ten years older than Cynthia, had lived with her mother in New York and seldom visited the Cape.

Cynthia laid the brush on the dresser. Had it been a crazy impulse to come here? Two weeks out of prison, barely enough money to live on for six months, not knowing what she could do or would do with her life. Should she have spent so much to rent this cottage, to rent a car? Was there any point to it? What did she hope to accomplish?

A needle in a haystack, she thought. Walking into the small parlor, she reflected that compared to Stuart's mansion, this house was tiny, but after years of confinement it seemed palatial. Outside the sea breeze was blowing the Bay into churning waves. Cynthia walked out on the porch, only vaguely aware of her throbbing wrist, hugging her arms against the chill. But, oh God, to breathe fresh clean air, to know that if she wanted to get up at dawn and walk the beach the way she had as a child, no one could stop her. The moon, three-quarters full, looking as though a wedge had been neatly sliced from it, made the water glisten, a silvery midnight blue. Where the moon did not touch it, the water looked dark and impenetrable.

Cynthia stared at the water as she thought about the night Stuart was shot. The summer she'd stayed at school taking extra courses, wanting to keep busy after her mother's sudden death three months earlier.

Stuart had phoned and invited her down for the weekend. 'I've been in Europe,' he said. 'I just heard. I'm so very sorry, Cindy.'

She'd come to his home because she knew that, self-centered and difficult as he was, in his own way Stuart had loved her mother and she wanted the feeling of sharing even a little of her overwhelming grief.

Stuart had been about sixty then, handsome with his white hair, vivid blue eyes, striking profile, military carriage. A successful businessman who'd turned a modest inheritance into $20 million, a man who could be charming but whose outbursts of anger drove away his wives, his friends, his employees.

That weekend the weather was cloudy and overcast, Stuart was moody and withdrawn. He'd told her that his housekeeper had quit, that he had a woman who came in for only a few hours each morning to tidy up.

Cynthia and Stuart had dinner at the Wianno Country Club on Friday night. He remarked a number of times upon how much she was growing to look like her mother. 'I should have had the brains to hang on to her.' He questioned her closely about her finances. 'Your mother loved to spend money. I bet she went through the settlement.'

The settlement had not been that generous. Cynthia remembered the quick flash of resentment that raced through her as she told him: 'You said you were sorry you didn't hang on to her. Well, you were right. If you hadn't criticized every dime she spent, she wouldn't have left you. She still loved you even afterward.'

That famous dark red had suffused Stuart's face. 'I invited you down because I feel somewhat responsible for you, young lady, and because I wanted to talk to you about your future. Don't you ever dare criticize me.'

That was when Cynthia had realized that someone was turning the corner of the house to the back porch and had probably over heard them. Saturday mid-afternoon. The beginning of the nightmare.

Stuart greeted the newcomer warmly and introduced them. Ned Creighton. 'Known Ned since he was born,' he said. 'How long ago is that, Ned?'

'Almost thirty years.' Ned had smiled over at Cynthia. 'We met one summer, Cynthia. You were about ten. You've done a lot of growing up.' His smile had been engaging.

She didn't remember but decided immediately that he'd probably come on one of those rare weekends when Lillian was present. Since Lillian, who hated her, never included her in anything, she was surprised she had even met Ned. Later, when Ned invited her for dinner and a ride on his new boat, Stuart had insisted she go. 'I've got some paperwork to do. Some things I want to go over with you tomorrow. Money. And my will, for example.' His expression had darkened.

She and Ned had dinner at the Captain's Table. He was lighthearted and amusing. 'I thought you deserved more than an unbroken weekend with Stuart. God, isn't he formidable? Used to scare me speechless when I was a kid.' His eyes crinkling, his sun-streaked hair contrasting with his china-blue eyes, his slender muscular body accentuated by the sports shirt, green linen jacket and white slacks, he'd been the personification of charm. He told Cynthia he was getting together investors to buy an old mansion in Barnstable and turn it into a restaurant. 'Great location. Could be fantastic. By this time next year maybe I'll be inviting you there for the best meal on the Cape.'

He asked about her own plans. 'I want to finish college. Stuart's been paying my way. He doesn't have to.

I think he was being so generous to me because he hoped to get my mother back, and now that will never happen. Stuart isn't one to be generous unless he's looking to get something back. Did you catch the remark about money and his will?'

Ned nodded. 'Yes. Good luck.'

Cynthia remembered laughing about the fact that this side of the Cape was unknown territory to her. From the Captain's Table they'd driven forty minutes to a private dock in the Cotuit area. It was in an isolated spot at the back of a house that seemed deserted.

Ned's boat was a twenty-two-foot Chris Craft.

'In a couple of years. I'll take you out on a yacht.' He had steered so far out into the Bay that the shoreline was barely visible. The night was overcast. The breeze was cool and filled with the scent of the sea. There were no other boats anywhere around. Ned dropped anchor. 'I think it's time for a nightcap.'

In the endless hours of her imprisonment Cynthia thought over and over again of that night. Ned opening champagne. Sitting across from her, smiling, re-filling her glass, agreeing with her that Cape Cod was a place that got into your bones. 'I've missed it so much,' Cynthia had confided. The fact that for the first time since her mother's death she was having fun. Telling him about her plans to become a commercial artist. His intelligent questions about where she'd look for a job. Her answer that it would probably be New York, that she didn't have any family now to hold her to Boston.

He'd asked about her relationship with Stuart. She'd told him that at the time of the divorce she'd hated him. 'I was only twelve. I realized how much my mother loved him, but she couldn't live with him. If you know him well you've probably seen his mood swings. He could be a fanatic. He'd spot something out of place in the house and shout at my mother, saying she didn't known how to train help. She was really beautiful, but they'd be going to an important dinner and he'd tell her he didn't like her dress. She changed from a happy, self-confident woman to someone who trembled when a door slammed. Oddly enough, he was always very pleasant to me. In fact, he wanted to adopt me. She wouldn't let him.'

'Have you seen very much of him for the last seven years?' Ned had asked.

'Not much. He lived in New York during the winter and traveled a lot. But he'd call and take me out to dinner two or three times a year. He always said, "If your mother would like to come, please tell her I'd be delighted." She never would, and I sometimes wonder if Stuart really wanted to see me or just get news about her. But he was the only person I ever knew as a father, so I was glad to see him and in a crazy way I was sorry for him.'

Then she'd said, 'It's getting late. Maybe we'd better start back.' But when Ned tried to turn on the motor there was no response. 'And the damn radio isn't hooked up,' he'd muttered. 'But listen, just relax. It's a nice night and I'll get it fixed somehow.'

It was nearly eleven when the motor finally turned over. By then Cynthia was starving because she'd only ordered a salad for dinner. When they docked she'd asked if they could stop for a hamburger.

'Why not get something at home?' Ned suggested impatiently.

'You just don't go messing around in Stuart's kitchen,' she answered, laughing.

He drove to a hamburger place. Blaring rock music could be heard from within. 'Wait in the car,' he said. Afterward Cynthia realized it was an order.

She'd rolled down the window and watched with amusement as a bulky woman struggled from the neighboring car and, not realizing Cynthia could hear, said aloud, 'Damn kids and that damn racket. Forty years on the Cape and the noise gets worse every day.'

At that point the woman had shoved her car door open and it banged against the side of Ned's Buick. The woman ducked her head into the open window. 'Say, I'm sorry about that. That rock-and-roll stuff makes me want to kill someone, but I don't take my violence out on other people's property.' She'd pulled her head out and examined the side of Ned's car. 'Not even a nick, I swear it.'

'I'm sure its fine,' Cynthia told her. She'd watched as the woman headed for the door of the hamburger joint. Mid- or late forties, chunky body, blunt-cut hair dyed an orange-red, shapeless blouse, elastic-waisted polyester slacks, a sturdy no-nonsense walk.

Ned was clearly annoyed when he came back, a cardboard container in his hand. 'Those damn kids can't make up their minds when they're giving an order. That is, if they have any minds.'

For some reason Cynthia decided not to tell him about the encounter with the woman. The mood of the evening had now changed. Ned gave her the container with the hamburger and brusquely said he wasn't hungry. He hadn't bought anything for himself.

It was a forty-five-minute drive along unfamiliar roads back to Dennis. When they reached Stuart's house, Ned pushed open the car door for her. 'It's been great, Cynthia,' he said quickly.

Puzzled at his rudeness in not walking her to the door and disappointed by his desire to get away, Cynthia had gone into the quiet house, noticed the light in Stuart's study, knocked on the partially open door and then looked inside. Stuart was sprawled on the floor near his desk, blood drenching his forehead, blood caked on his face, blood matted on the carpet around him. She'd rushed to him, thinking he might have had a stroke and fallen. When she put her hand on his head and brushed his hair back, she saw the bullet wounds in his forehead, then the gun beside his hand. In a daze she picked up the gun, laid it on the desk and dialed the police. 'I think my stepfather, Stuart Richards, has committed suicide.' She was sitting beside his body in shock when the police arrived.

When they checked her story, Ned swore he had not been with her after eight o'clock. 'I took her home directly from the Captain's Table,' he said. 'Her stepfather wanted to talk to her about family business.'

Cynthia shook her head. No more remembering that night tonight. It was time to let the peace of this place fill her soul, time to got to bed. She'd leave the windows open wide so that as the night wind strengthened it would race through the room, rippling the pillowcases, compelling her in sleep to pull the covers closer around her. She'd wake up early and walk on the beach, feel the wet sand under her feet and look for shells as she had when she was a child. Tomorrow. She would give herself tomorrow morning to attempt to fill the wellsprings of her being and then she would begin the quest that was probably hopeless, the quest for the one person who would know she had told the truth.

The next morning, as Alvirah prepared breakfast, Willy drove to get the morning papers. He returned with them and a bag of steaming-hot blueberry muffins. 'I asked around,' he told a delighted Alvirah. 'Everyone said to go to Just Desserts next to the post office for the best muffins on the Cape.'

They ate at the picnic table on the deck. As she nibbled on her second blueberry muffin, Alvirah studied the early-morning joggers on the beach. 'Look, there she is!'

'There who is?'

'Cynthia Lathem. She's been gone at least an hour and a half. I bet she's starving.'

When Cynthia ascended the steps from the beach to her deck she was met by a beaming Alvirah, who linked her arm in Cynthia's. 'I make the best coffee and squeezed fresh orange juice. And wait till you taste the blueberry muffins.'

'I really don't want . . .' Cynthia tried to pull back but was propelled across the lawn. Willy jumped up to pull out a bench for her.

'How's your wrist?' he asked. 'Alvirah's been real upset that you sprained it when she went over to visit.'

Cynthia realized that her mounting irritation was being overcome by the genuine warmth she saw on both their faces. Willy – with his rounded cheeks, strong, pleasant expression and thick mane of white hair – reminded her of Tip O'Neill. She told him that.

Willy beamed. 'Fellow just remarked that in the bakery. Only difference is that while Tip was *speaker* of the house I was *savior* of the *outhouse*. I'm a retired plumber.'

As Cynthia sipped the fresh orange juice and the coffee and picked at the muffin, she listened with disbelief, then awe, as Alvirah told her about winning the lottery, going to Cypress Point Spa and helping to track down a murderer, then going on an Alaskan cruise and figuring out who killed the man who sat next to her at the community table.

She accepted a second cup of coffee. 'You've told me all this for a reason, haven't you?' Cynthia said. 'You recognized me yesterday, didn't you?'

Alvirah became serious. 'Yes.'

Cynthia pushed back her chair. 'You've been very kind, and I think you want to help me, but the best way you can do that is to leave me alone.'

Alvirah watched the slender young figure walk between the two cottages. 'She got a little sun this morning,' she observed. 'Very becoming. When she fills out a little, she'll be a beautiful girl.'

'You may as well plan on getting the sun too,' Willy observed. 'You heard her.'

'Oh, forget it. Once Charley sends the files on her case I'll figure out a way to help her.'

'Oh my God,' Willy moaned. 'I might have known. Here we go again.'

'I don't know how Charley does it,' Alvirah sighed a few hours later. The overnight express envelope had arrived just as they finished breakfast. 'He sent everything except a transcript of the trial and he'll get that in the next couple of days.' Alvirah pursed her lips.

Willy was reclining on the padded chaise he had claimed as his own and had almost finished reading the sports section of the fourth newspaper he had purchased. 'I'm about ready to give up on the Mets for a pennant,' he commented sadly.

Alvirah did not hear him. 'Willy,' she said in the voice that told him she was going to ask an important question, 'do you think that girl is crazy?'

Willy knew who she meant. 'I think she's a nice kid. I feel sorry for her.'

'I agree. Do you think she's intelligent?'

'Bright as a button. You can tell.'

'You're right. Well, I just read all these newspaper stories about that case again. Now why would an intelligent young woman, even at nineteen, come up with a cock-and-bull story about where she was when her stepfather was murdered? Wouldn't she have to

103

be crazy or stupid to expect a stranger to lie for her?' Alvirah shook her head '*Somebody's* lying, that's perfectly clear, and I'll bet my bottom dollar it isn't Cynthia. So why is she here?' Now her voice became triumphant. 'I'll tell you why, Willy. She *still* wants to find out what happened to Stuart Richards that night and she wants to clear her name.' Alvirah beamed. 'Isn't it lucky I'm here to help her?'

Willy laid down the sports page. 'Oh my God,' he murmured again.

The long and peaceful night's sleep followed by the early-morning walk had begun to clear the emotional paralysis that Cynthia had experienced from the moment she'd heard the jury pronounce the verdict of 'Guilty' twelve years earlier. Now as she showered and dressed she reflected that these past years had been a nightmare in which she had managed to survive only by freezing her emotions. She had been a model prisoner. She had kept to herself, resisting friendships. She had taken whatever jailhouse college courses were offered. She had graduated from working in the laundry and the kitchen to desk assignments in the library and assistant teaching in the art class. And after a while when the awful reality of what had happened finally set in, she had begun to draw. The face of the woman in the parking lot. The hamburger stand. Ned's boat. Every detail she could force from her memory. When she was finished she had pictures of a hamburger place that could be found anywhere in the United States, a boat that looked like any Chris Craft of that year. The woman was a littler clearer but not much. It had been dark. Their encounter had only taken seconds. But the woman was her only hope.

The prosecutor's summation at the end of the trial: 'Ladies and Gentlemen of the Jury, Cynthia Lathem returned to the home of Stuart Richards sometime between eight and eight-thirty P.M. on the night of August 2, 1976. She went into her stepfather's study. That very afternoon Stuart Richards had told Cynthia he was going to change his will. Ned Creighton overheard that conversation, overheard Cynthia and Stuart quarreling. Vera Smith, the waitress at the Captain's Table, overheard Cynthia tell Ned that she would have to drop out of school if her stepfather refused to continue paying for her education.

'Cynthia Lathem returned to the Richards' mansion that night, angry and worried. She went into that study and confronted Stuart Richards. He was a man who enjoyed upsetting the people around him. He *had* changed his will. He would have saved his life if he had told his stepdaughter that instead of a few thousand dollars, he was leaving half his fortune to her. Instead he teased her too long. And the anger she'd harbored for the way he had treated her mother, the anger that rose in her at the thought of having to leave school, at being turned out into the world virtually penniless, made her go to the armoire where she knew he kept a gun, take out that gun and fire three shots point-blank into the forehead of the man who loved her enough to make her an heiress.

'It is irony. It is tragedy. It is also murder. Cynthia begged Ned Creighton to say she had spent the evening with him on his boat. No one saw them out on the boat. She talks about shopping at a hamburger stand. But she doesn't know where it is. She admits she never entered it. She talks about a stranger with orange-red hair to whom she spoke in a parking lot. With all the publicity this case has engendered, why didn't that woman come forward? You know the reason. Because she doesn't exist. Because like the hamburger stand and the hours spent in a boat on

Cape Cod Bay, she is a figment of Cynthia Lathem's imagination.'

Cynthia had read the transcript of the trial so often that she had the district attorney's summation committed to memory. 'But the woman did exist,' Cynthia said aloud. 'She does exist.' For the next six months, with the little insurance left her by her mother she was going to try to find that woman. She might be dead by now, or moved to California, Cynthia thought as she brushed her hair and twisted it into a chignon.

The bedroom of the cottage faced the sea. Cynthia walked to the sliding door and pulled it open. On the beach below she could see couples walking with children. If she was ever to have a normal life, a husband, a child of her own, she had to clear her name.

Jeff Knight. She had met him last year when he came to do a series of television interviews with women in prison. He'd invited her to participate, and she'd flatly refused. He'd persisted, his strong intelligent face filled with concern. 'Don't you understand, Cynthia, this program is going to be watched by a couple of million people in New England. The woman who saw you that night could be one of those people.'

That was why she had gone on the program, answered his questions, told about the night Stuart died, held up the shadowy sketch of the woman she had spoken with, the sketch of the hamburger stand. And no one had come forward. From New York Lillian issued a statement saying that the truth had been told at the trial and she would have no further comment. Ned Creighton, now the owner of the Mooncusser, a popular restaurant in Barnstable, repeated how very, very sorry he was for Cynthia.

After the program, Jeff kept coming to see her on visiting days. Only those visits had kept her from total despair when the program produced no results. He would always arrive a little rumpled-looking, his wide shoulders straining at his jacket, his unsettled dark-brown hair curling on his forehead, his brown eyes intense and kind, his long legs never able to find enough room in the cramped visiting area of the prison. When he asked her to marry him after her release she told him to forget her. He was already getting bids from the networks. He didn't need a convicted murderer in his life.

But what if I weren't a convicted murderer, Cynthia thought as she turned away from the window. She went over to the maple dresser, reached for her pocket book and went outside to her rented car.

It was early evening before she returned to Dennis. The frustration of the wasted hours had finally brought tears to her eyes. She let them run down her cheeks unchecked. She'd driven to Cotuit, walked around the main street, inquired of the bookstore owner – who seemed to be a longtime native – about a hamburger stand that was a teenage hang-out. Where would she be likely to find one? The answer, with a shrug, was, 'They come and go. A developer picks up property and builds a shopping center or condominiums and the hamburger stand is out.' She'd gone to the Town Hall to try to find records of food-service licenses issued or renewed in 1977. Two hamburger-type places were still in business. The third had been converted or torn down. None of them stirred her memory. And of course she couldn't even be sure they had been in Cotuit. Ned might have been lying about that too. And how do you ask strangers if they know a middle-aged woman with orange-red hair and a chunky build who had lived or summered on the Cape for forty years and hated rock-and-roll music?

As she drove through Dennis, Cynthia impulsively ignored the turn to the cottage and again drove past the Richards' home. As she was passing, a slender blonde woman came down the steps of the mansion. Even from this distance she knew it was Lillian. Cynthia slowed the car to a crawl, but when Lillian looked in her direction quickly accelerated and returned to the cottage. As she was turning the key in the lock she heard the phone ring. It rang ten times before it stopped. It had to be Jeff, and she didn't want to talk to him. A few minutes later it rang again. It was obvious that if Jeff had the number he wouldn't give up trying to reach her.

Cynthia picked up the receiver. 'Hello.'

'My finger is getting very tired pushing buttons,' Jeff said. 'Nice trick of yours, just disappearing like that.'

'How did you find me?'

'It wasn't hard. I knew you'd head for the Cape like a homing pigeon, and your parole officer confirmed it.'

She could see him leaning back in his chair, twirling a pencil, the seriousness in his eyes belying the lightness of his tone. 'Jeff, forget about me, please. Do us both a favor.'

'Negative. Cindy, I understand. But unless you can find that woman you spoke to there's no hope of proving your innocence. And believe me, honey, I tried to find her. When I did the program, I sent out investigators I never told you about. If they couldn't find her, you won't be able to. Cindy, I love you. You know you're innocent: I know your innocent. Ned Creighton lied, but we'll never be able to prove it.'

Cindy closed her eyes, knowing that what Jeff said was true.

'Cindy, give it all up. Pack your bag. Drive back here. I'll pick you up at your place at eight o'clock tonight.'

Her place. The furnished room the parole officer

had helped her select. *Meet my girl-friend. She just got out of prison. What did your mother do before she got married? She was in jail?*

'Good-bye, Jeff,' Cynthia said. She broke the connection, left the phone off the hook and turned her back to it.

Alvirah had observed Cynthia's return but did not attempt to contact her. In the afternoon, Willy had gone out on a half-day charter boat and returned triumphantly with two bluefish. During his absence, Alvirah studied the newspaper clippings of the Stuart Richards' murder case. At Cypress Point Spa she had learned the value of airing her opinions into a recorder. That afternoon she kept her recorder busy.

'The crux of this case is why did Ned Creighton lie? He hardly knew Cynthia. Why did he set her up to take the blame for Stuart Richards' death? Stuart Richards had a lot of enemies. Ned's father at one time had business dealings with Stuart and they'd had a falling out, but Ned was only a kid at that time. Ned was a friend of Lillian Richards. Lillian swore that she didn't know that her father was going to change his will, that she'd always known she would get half his estate and that the other half was going to Dartmouth College. She said that she knew he was upset when Dartmouth decided to accept women students but didn't know he was upset enough to change his will and leave the Dartmouth money to Cynthia.'

Alvirah turned off the recorder. It certainly must have occurred to someone that when Cynthia was found guilty of murdering her stepfather, she would lose his inheritance and Lillian would receive everything. Lillian had married somebody from New York shortly after the trial was over. She'd been divorced three times since then. So it didn't look as though Ned and she had ever had any romance going. That left only the restaurant. Who were Ned's backers?

Willy came in from the deck carrying the bluefish fillets he'd prepared. 'Still at it?' he asked.

'Uh-huh.' Alvirah picked up one of the clippings. 'Orange-red hair, chunky build, in her late forties. Would you say that description might have fit me twelve years ago?'

'Now you know I would never call you chunky,' Willy protested.

'I didn't say you would. I'll be right back. I want to talk to Cynthia. I saw her coming in a few minutes ago.'

The next afternoon after having packed Willy off on another charter fishing boat. Alvirah attached her star-burst pin to her new purple print dress and drove with Cynthia to the Mooncusser Restaurant in Barnstable. Along the way Alvirah coached her. 'Now remember, if he's there, point him out to me right away. I'll keep staring at him. He'll recognize you. He's bound to come over. You known what to say, don't you?'

'I do.' Was it possible? Cynthia wondered. Would Ned believe them?

The restaurant was an impressive white colonial-style building with a long, winding driveway. Alvirah took in the building, the exquisitely landscaped property that extended to the water. 'Very, very ex-pensive,' she said to Cynthia. 'He didn't start this place on a shoestring.'

The interior was decorated in Wedgwood blue and white. The paintings on the wall were fine ones. For twenty years – until she and Willy hit the lottery – Alvirah had cleaned every Tuesday for Mrs. Rawlings, and her house was one big museum. Mrs. Rawlings enjoyed recounting the history of each painting, how much she'd paid for it then and, gleefully, how much it was worth right now. Alvirah often thought that with a little practice she could probably be a tour guide at an art museum. 'Observe the use of lightning, the splendid details of sunrays brightening the dust on the table.' She had the Rawlings' spiel down pat.

Knowing Cynthia was nervous, Alvirah tried to distract her by telling her about Mrs. Rawlings after the maître d'hôtel escorted them to a window table.

Cynthia felt a reluctant smile come to her lips as Alvirah told her that with all her money, Mrs. Rawlings never once gave her so much as a postcard at Christmas. 'Meanest, cheapest old biddy in the world, but I felt kind of sorry for her,' Alvirah said. 'No one else would work for her. But when my time comes, I intend to point out to the Lord that I get a lot of Rawlings points in my plus column.'

'If this idea works, you get a lot of Lathem points in your plus column,' Cynthia said.

'You bet I do. Now don't lose that smile. You've got to look like the cat who ate the canary, is he here?'

'I haven't seen him yet.'

'Good. When that stuffed shirt comes back with the menu, ask for him.'

The maître d' was approaching them, a professional smile on his bland face. 'May I offer you a beverage?'

'Yes. Two glasses of white wine, and is Mr. Creighton here?' Cynthia asked.

'I believe he's in the kitchen speaking with the chef.'

'I'm an old friend,' Cynthia said. 'Ask him to drop by when he's free.'

'Certainly.'

'You could be an actress,' Alvirah whispered, holding the menu in front of her face. She always felt that you had to be so careful because someone might be able to read lips.' And I'm glad I made you buy that outfit this morning. What you had in your closet was hopeless.'

111

Cynthia was wearing a short lemon-coloured linen jacket and a black linen skirt. A splashy yellow, black and white silk scarf was dramatically tied on one shoulder. Alvirah had also escorted her to the beauty parlor. Now Cynthia's collar-length hair was blown soft and loose around her face. A light-beige foundation covered her abnormal paleness and returned color to her wide hazel eyes. 'You're gorgeous,' Alvirah said.

Regretfully Alvirah had undergone a different metamorphosis. She'd had Sassoon hair color changed back to its old range-red and cut unevenly. She'd also had the tips removed from her nails and left them unpolished. After helping Cynthia select the yellow and black outfit, she'd gone to the sale rack where for very good reasons the purple print she was wearing had been reduced to $10. The fact that it was a size too small for her accentuated the bulges that Willy always explained were only nature's way of padding us for the last big fall.

When Cynthia protested the desecration of her nails and hairdo, Alvirah simply said, 'Every time you talked about that woman, the missing witness, you said she was chunky, had dyed red hair and was dressed like someone who shopped from a pushcart. I've gotta be believable.'

'I said her outfit looked inexpensive,' Cynthia corrected.

'Same thing.'

Now Alvirah watched as Cynthia's smile faded. 'He's coming?' she asked quickly.

Cynthia nodded.

'Smile at me. Come on. Relax. Don't show him you're nervous.'

Cynthia rewarded her with a warm smile and leaned her elbows lightly on the table.

A man was standing over them. Beads of perspiration were forming on his forehead. He moistened his lips. 'Cynthia, how good to see you.' He reached for her hand.

Alvirah studied him intently. Not bad-looking in a weak kind of way. Narrow eyes almost lost in puffy flesh. He was a good twenty pounds heavier than the pictures in the files. The kind who are handsome as kids and after that it's all downhill.

'Is it good to see me, Ned?' Cynthia asked, still smiling.

'That's him,' Alvirah announced emphatically. 'I'm absolutely sure. He was ahead of me on the line in the hamburger joint. I noticed him 'cause he was sore as hell that the kids in front were hemming and hawing about what they wanted on their burgers.'

'What are you talking about?' Ned Creighton demanded.

'Why don't you sit down, Ned?' Cynthia said. 'I know this is your place, but I still feel as though I should entertain you. After all, you did buy me dinner one night years ago.'

Good girl, Alvirah thought. 'I'm absolutely sure it was you that night even though you've put on weight,' she snapped indignantly to Creighton. 'It's a crying shame that because of your lies this girl had to spend twelve years of her life in prison.'

The smile vanished from Cynthia's face. 'Twelve years, six months and ten days,' she corrected. 'All my twenties when I should have been finishing college, getting my first job, dating.'

Ned Creighton's face hardened. 'You're bluffing. This is a cheap trick.'

The waiter arrived with two glasses of wine and placed them before Cynthia and Alvirah. 'Mr. Creighton?'

113

Creighton glared at him. 'Nothing.'

'This is really a lovely place, Ned,' Cynthia said quietly. 'An awful lot of money must have gone into it. Where did you get it? From Lillian? My share of Stuart Richards' estate was nearly ten million dollars. How much did she give you?' She did not wait for an answer. 'Ned, this woman is the witness I could never find. She remembers talking to me that night. Nobody believed me when I told them about someone slamming her car door against the side of your car. But she remembers doing it. And she remembers seeing you very well. All her life she's kept a daily dairy. That night she wrote about what happened in the parking lot.'

As she kept nodding her head in agreement, Alvirah studied Ned's face. He's getting rattled, she thought, but he's not convinced. It was time for her to take over. 'I left the Cape the very next day,' she said. 'I live in Arizona. My husband was sick, real sick. That's why we never did come back. I lost him last year.' Sorry, Willy, she thought, but this is important. 'Then last week I was watching television, and you know how boring television usually is in the summer. You could have knocked me over with a feather when I saw a rerun of that show about women in prison and then my own picture right there on the screen.'

Cynthia reached for the envelope she had placed beside her chair. 'This is the picture I drew of the woman I'd spoken to in the parking lot.'

Ned Creighton reached for it.

'I'll hold it,' Cynthia said.

The sketch showed a woman's face framed by an open car window. The features were shadowy and the background was dark, but the likeness to Alvirah was astonishing.

Cynthia pushed back her chair. Alvirah rose with

her. 'You can't give me back twelve years. I know what you're thinking. Even with this proof, a jury might not believe me. It didn't believe me twelve years ago. But it might, it just might. And I don't think you should take that chance. Ned, I think you'd better talk it over with whoever paid you to set me up that night and tell them that I want ten million dollars. That's my rightful share of Stuart's estate.'

'You're crazy.' Anger had driven the fear from Ned Creighton's face.

'Am I? I don't think so.' Cynthia reached into her pocket. 'Here's my address and phone number. Alvirah is staying with me. Call me by seven tonight. If I don't hear from you, I'm hiring a lawyer and getting my case reopened.' She threw a $10 bill on the table. 'That should pay for the wine. I'm still paying for that dinner you bought me.'

She walked rapidly from the restaurant, Alvirah a step behind her. Alvirah was aware of the buzz from diners at the other tables. They know something's up, she thought. Good.

She and Cynthia did not speak until they were in the car. Then Cynthia asked shakily, 'How was I?'

'Great.'

'Alvirah, it won't work. If they check the sketch that Jeff showed on the program, they'll see all the details I added to make it look like you.'

'They haven't got time to do that. Are you sure you saw your stepsister yesterday at the Richards' house?'

'Absolutely.'

'Then my guess is that Ned Creighton is talking to her now.'

Cynthia drove automatically, not seeing the sunny brightness of the afternoon. 'Stuart was despised by a lot of people. Why are you so sure Lillian is involved?'

Alvirah unfastened the zipper on the purple print.

'This dress is so tight I swear I'm gonna choke.' Ruefully she ran her hand through her erratically chopped hair. 'It'll take an army of Sassoons to put me back together after this. I guess I'll have to go back to Cypress Point Spa. What did you ask? Oh, Lillian. She *has* to be involved. Look at it this way. Your stepfather had a lot of people who hated his guts, but they wouldn't need a Ned Creighton to set you up. Lillian always knew her father was leaving half of his money to Dartmouth College. Right?'

'Yes.' Cynthia turned down the road that led to the cottages.

'I don't care how many people might have *hated* your stepfather, Lillian was the only one who *benefited* by you being set up to be found guilty of his murder. She knew Ned. Ned was trying to raise money to open a restaurant. Her father must have told her he was leaving half his fortune to you instead of Dartmouth. She always hated you. You told me that. So she makes a deal with Ned. He takes you out on his boat and pretends that it breaks down. Somebody kills Stuart Richards. Lillian had an alibi. She was in New York. She probably hired someone to kill her father. You almost spoiled everything that night by insisting on having a hamburger. And Ned didn't know you'd spoken to anyone. They must have been plenty scared that that witness would show up.'

'Suppose someone recognized him that night and said they'd seen him buying the burger?'

'In that case he'd have said that he went out on his boat and stopped afterwards for a hamburger and you were so desperate for an alibi you begged him to say you were with him. But no one did come forward.'

'It sounds so risky,' Cynthia protested.

'Not risky. Simple,' Alvirah corrected. 'Buhlieve me, I've studied up on this a lot. You'd be amazed in how many cases the one who commits the murder is the chief mourner at the funeral. It's a fact.'

They had arrived back at the cottages. 'What now?' Cynthia asked.

'Now we go to your place and wait for your stepsister to phone.' Alvirah shook her head at Cynthia. 'You still don't believe me. Wait and see. I'll make us a nice cup of tea. It's too bad Creighton showed up before we had lunch. That was a good menu.'

They were eating tuna-salad sandwiches on the deck of Cynthia's cottage when the phone rang. 'Lillian for you,' Alvirah said. She followed Cynthia into the kitchen and waited as Cynthia answered the call.

'Hello.' Cynthia's voice was almost a whisper. Alvirah watched as the color drained from her face. 'Hello, Lillian.'

Alvirah squeezed Cynthia's arm and nodded her head vigorously.

'Yes. Lillian, I just saw Ned. No, I'm not joking. I don't see anything funny about this. Yes. I'll come over tonight. Don't bother about dinner. Your presence has a way of making my throat close. And, Lillian, I told Ned what I want. I won't change my mind.'

Cynthia hung up and sank into a chair. 'Alvirah, Lillian said that my accusation was ridiculous but that she knows her father could drive anyone to the point of losing control. She's smart.'

'That doesn't help us clear your name. I'll give you my sunburst pin. You've got to get her to admit that you had absolutely nothing to do with the murder, that she set Ned up to trap you. What time did you tell her you'd go over to her house?'

'Eight o'clock. Ned will be with her.'

'Fine. Willy will go with you. He'll be on the floor in the back seat of the car. For a big man he can roll himself into a beach ball. He'll keep an eye on you. They

117

certainly won't try anything in that house. It would be too risky.' Alvirah unfastened her sunburst pin. 'Next to Willy, this is my greatest treasure,' she said. 'Now I'll show you how to use it.'

Throughout the afternoon, Alvirah coached Cynthia on what to say to her stepsister. 'She's got to be the one who put up the money for the restaurant. Probably through some sham investment companies. Tell her unless she pays up, you're going to contact a top accountant you know who used to work for the government.'

'She knows I don't have any money.'

'She doesn't know who might have taken an interest in your case. That fellow who did the program on women in prison did, right?'

'Yes, Jeff took an interest.'

Alvirah's eyes narrowed, then sparked. 'Something between you and Jeff?'

'If I'm exonerated for Stuart Richards' death, yes. If I'm not, there'll never be anything between Jeff and me or anyone else and me.'

At six o'clock the phone rang again. Alvirah said, 'I'll answer. Let them know I'm right here with you.' Her booming 'Hello' was followed by a warm greeting. 'Jeff, we were just talking about you. Cynthia is right here. My, what a pretty girl. You should see her new outfit. She's been telling me all about you. Wait. I'll put her on.'

Alvirah frankly listened in as Cynthia explained, 'Alvirah rents the next cottage. She's helping me. No, I'm not coming back. Yes, there is a reason to stay here. Tonight just maybe I'll be able to get proof I wasn't guilty of Stuart's death. No, don't come down. I don't want to see you, Jeff, not now . . . Jeff, yes, yes, I love you. Yes, if I clear my name, I'll marry you.'

When Cynthia hung up she was close to tears. 'Alvirah, I want to have a life with him so much. You know

118

what he just said? He quoted the *Highwayman*. He said, "I'll come to you by moonlight though hell should bar the way."'

'I like him,' Alvirah said flatly. 'I can read a person from his voice on the phone. Is he coming tonight? I don't want you getting upset or being talked out of this.'

'No. He's been made anchorman for the ten o'clock news. But I bet anything he drives down tomorrow.'

'We'll have to see about that. The more people in this the more chance of having Ned and Lillian smell a rat.' Alvirah glanced out the window. 'Oh, look, here comes Willy. Stars above, he caught more of those darn bluefish. They give me heartburn, but I'd never tell him. Whenever he goes fishing I keep a package of Tums in my pocket. Oh, well.'

She opened the door for a beaming Willy who was proudly holding a line from which two limp bluefish dangled forlornly. Willy's smile vanished as he took in Alvirah's bright-red mop of unruly hair and the purple print dress that squeezed her body into rolls of flesh. 'Aw, nuts,' he said. 'How come they took back the lottery money?'

At seven-thirty, after having dined on Willy's latest catch, Alvirah placed a cup of tea in front of Cynthia. 'You haven't eaten a thing,' she said. 'You've got to eat to keep your brain clear. Now, have you got it all straight?'

Cynthia fingered the sunburst pin. 'I think so. It seems clear.'

'Remember, money had to have changed hands between those two – and I don't care how clever they were, it can be traced. If they agree to pay you, offer to come down in price if they'll give you the satisfaction of admitting the truth. Got it?'

'Got it.'

119

At seven-fifty Cynthia drove down the winding lane with Willy on the floor of the back seat.

The brilliantly sunny day had turned into a cloudy evening. Alvirah walked through the cottage to the back deck. Wind was whipping the bay into a frenzy of waves that slammed onto the beach. The rumbling of thunder could be heard in the distance. The temperature had plummeted and suddenly it felt more like October than August. Shivering, she debated about going next door to her cottage and getting a sweater, then decided against it. In case anyone phoned, she wanted to be right here.

She made a second cup of tea for herself and settled at the dinette table, her back to the door leading from the deck, then began writing a first draft of the article she was sure she would soon be sending to the *New York Globe*. Cynthia Lathem, who was nineteen years old when she was sentenced to a term of twelve years in prison for a murder she did not commit, can now prove her innocence.

From behind her a voice, 'Oh, I don't think that's going to happen.'

Alvirah swirled around and stared up into the grim, angry face of Ned Creighton.

Cynthia waited on the porch steps of the Richards' mansion. Through the handsome mahogany door she could hear the faint sound of chimes. She had the incongruous thought that she still had her own key to this place and she wondered if Lillian had changed the locks.

The door swung open. Lillian was standing in the wide hallway, light from the overhead Tiffany lamp accentuating her high cheekbones, wide blue eyes, silvery blonde hair. Cynthia felt a chill race through her body. In these twelve years, Lillian had become a clone of Stuart Richards. Smaller of course. Younger, but still a feminine version of his outstanding looks. And with that same hint of cruelty around the eyes.

'Come in, Cynthia.' Lillian's voice hadn't changed. Clear, well-bred, but with that familiar sharp, angry undertone that had always characterized Stuart Richards' speech.

Silently Cynthia followed Lillian down the hallway. The living room was dimly lighted. It looked very much as she remembered it. The placement of the furniture, the Oriental carpets, the painting over the fireplace – all were the same. The baronial dining room on the left still had the unused appearance that had always characterized it. They had usually eaten in the small dining room off the library.

She had expected that Lillian would take her to the library. Instead Lillian went directly back to the study where Stuart had died. Cynthia narrowed her lips, felt for the sunburst pin. Was this a way of intimidating her? she wondered.

Lillian sat behind the massive desk.

Cynthia thought again of the night she'd come into this room and found Stuart sprawled on the carpet beside that desk. She knew her hands were clammy. Perspiration was forming on her forehead. Outside she could hear the wind wailing as it increased in velocity.

Lillian folded her hands and looked up at Cynthia. 'You might as well sit down.'

Cynthia bit her lip. The rest of her life would be determined by what she said in these next minutes. 'I think I'm the one who should suggest the seating arrangements,' she told Lillian. 'Your father did leave this house to me. When you phoned, you talked about a settlement. Don't play games now. And don't try to intimidate me. Prison took all that shyness out of me. I promise you that. Where is Ned?'

'He'll be along any minute. Cynthia, those accusations you made to him are insane. You know that.'

'I thought I had come here to discuss receiving my share of Stuart's estate.'

'You came here because I am sorry for you and because I want to give you a chance to go away somewhere and begin a new life. I'm prepared to set up a trust fund that will give you a monthly income. Another woman wouldn't be so generous to her father's murderer.'

Cynthia stared at Lillian, taking in the contempt in her eyes, the icy calm of her demeanor. She had to break that calm. She walked over to the window and looked out. The rain was beating against the house. Claps of thunder shattered the silence in the room. 'I wonder what Ned would have done that night to keep me out of the house if it had been raining like this,' she said. 'The weather worked for him, didn't it? Warm and cloudy. No other boats nearby. Only that one witness, and now I've found her. Didn't Ned tell you that she positively identified him?'

'How many people would believe that anyone could recognize a stranger after nearly thirteen years? Cynthia, I don't know whom you've hired for this charade, but I'm warning you – drop it. Accept my offer, or I'll call the police and have you arrested for harassment. Don't forget it's very easy to get a criminal's parole revoked.'

'A *criminal's* parole. I agree. But I'm not a criminal, and you know it.' Cynthia walked over to the Jacobean armoire and pulled open the top drawer. 'I knew Stuart kept a gun here. But you certainly knew it too. You claimed he had never told you that he'd changed his will and was leaving the Dartmouth half of his estate to me. But you were lying. If Stuart sent for me to tell me about his will, he certainly didn't hide what he was doing from you.'

'He did *not* tell me. I hadn't seen him for three months.'

'You may not have seen him, but you spoke to him, didn't you? You could have put up with Dartmouth getting half his fortune but couldn't stand the idea of splitting the money with me. You hated me for the years I lived in this house, for the fact that he liked me. And you two always clashed. You've got the same vile temper he had.'

Lillian stood up. 'You don't know what you're talking about.'

Cynthia slammed the drawer shut. 'Oh, yes, I do. And every fact that convicted me will convict you. I had a key to this house. You had a key. There was no sign of struggle. I don't think you sent anyone to murder him. I think you did it yourself. Stuart had a panic button on his desk. He didn't push it. He never thought his own daughter would harm him. Why did Ned just *happen* to stop by that afternoon? You knew Stuart had invited me here for the weekend. You knew that he'd encourage me to go out with Ned. Stuart liked company and then he liked to be alone. Maybe Ned hasn't made it clear to you. The witness I found keeps a diary. She showed it to me. She'd been writing in it every night since she was twenty. There was no way that entry could have been doctored. She described me. She described Ned's car. She even wrote about the noisy kids on line and how impatient everyone was with them.'

I'm getting to her, Cynthia thought. Lillian's face was pale. Her throat was closing convulsively. Deliberately Cynthia walked back to the desk so that the sunburst pin was pointed directly at Lillian. 'You played it smart, didn't you?' she asked. 'Ned didn't start pouring money into that restaurant until after I was safely in prison. And I'm sure that on the surface

123

he has some respectable investors. But today the government is awfully good at getting to the source of laundered money. *Your* money, Lillian.'

'You'll never prove it.' But Lillian's voice had become shrill.

Oh God. If I can just get her to admit it, Cynthia thought. She grasped the edge of the desk with clenched hands and leaned forward. 'Possibly not. But don't take the chance. Let me tell you how it feels to be fingerprinted and handcuffed. How it feels to sit next to a lawyer and hear the district attorney accuse you of murder. How it feels to study the faces of the jury. Jurors are ordinary-looking people. Old. Young. Black. White. Well-dressed. Shabby. But they hold the rest of your life in their hands. And, Lillian, you won't like it. The waiting. The damning evidence that fits you much more than it ever fitted me. You don't have the temperament or the guts to go through it.'

Lillian stood up. 'Bear in mind there were a lot of taxes when the estate was settled. How much do you want?'

'You should have stayed in Arizona,' Ned Creighton said to Alvirah. The gun he was holding was pointed at her chest. Alvirah sat at the dinette table measuring her chances to escape. There were none. He had believed her story his afternoon and now he had to kill her. Alvirah had the fleeting thought that she'd always known she would have made a wonderful actress. Should she warn him her husband would be home any minute? No. At the restaurant she'd told him she was a widow. How long would Willy and Cynthia be? Too long. Lillian wouldn't let Cynthia go until she was sure there was no witness alive, but maybe if she kept him talking, she'd think of something. 'How much did you get for your part in the murder?' she asked.

124

Ned Creighton smiled, a thin sneering movement of his mouth. 'Three million. Just enough to start a classy restaurant.'

Alvirah mourned the fact that she had lent her sunburst pin to Cynthia. Proof. Absolute, positive proof and she wasn't able to record it. And if anything happened to her no one would know. Mark my words, she thought. If I get out of this, I'm going to have Charley Evans get me a backup pin. Maybe that one should be silver.

Creighton waved the pistol. 'Get up.'

Alvirah pushed back the chair, leaned her hands on the table. The sugar bowl was in front of her. Did she dare try to throw it at him? She knew her aim was good, but a gun was faster than a sugar bowl.

'Go into the living room.' As she walked around the table, Creighton reached over, grabbed her notes and the beginning of her article and stuffed them in his pocket.

There was a wooden rocking chair next to the fireplace. Creighton pointed to it. 'Sit down right there.'

Alvirah sat down heavily. Ned's gun was still trained on her. If she tipped the rocker forward and landed on him, could she get away from him? Creighton reached for a narrow key dangling from the mantel. Leaning over, he inserted it in a cylinder in one of the bricks and turned it. The hissing sound of gas spurted from the fireplace. He straightened up. From a matchbox on the mantel he extracted a long safety match, scratched it on the brick, blew out the flame that flared from it and tossed it onto the hearth. 'It's getting cold,' he said. 'You decided to light a fire. You turned on the jet. You threw in a match, but it didn't take. When you bent down to turn off the jet and start again you lost your balance and fell. Your head struck the stone mantel and you lost consciousness. A terrible accident

125

for such a nice woman. Cynthia will be very upset when she finds you.'

The smell of gas was permeating the room. Alvirah tried to tilt the rocker forward. She had to take the chance of butting Creighton with her head and making him drop the gun. She was too late. A vise-like grip on her shoulders. The sense of being pulled forward. The side of her head slamming against the stone hearth. As she lost consciousness, Alvirah was aware of the sickening smell of gas filling her nostrils.

'Here's Ned now,' Lillian said calmly at the sound of door chimes. 'I'll let him in.'

Cynthia waited. Lillian still had not admitted anything. Could she get Ned Creighton to incriminate himself? She felt like a tightrope walker on a slippery wire trying to inch her way across a chasm. If she failed, the rest of her life wouldn't be worth living.

Creighton was following Lillian into the room. 'Cynthia.' His nod was impersonal, not unpleasant. He pulled up a chair beside the desk where Lillian had an open file of printouts.

'I'm just giving Cynthia an idea of how much the estate shrank after the taxes had been settled,' Lillian told Creighton. 'Then we'll estimate her share.'

'Don't deduct whatever you paid Ned from what is rightfully mine.' Cynthia said. She saw the angry look Ned shot at Lillian. 'Oh, please,' she snapped, 'among the three of us, let's say it straight.'

Lillian said coldly, 'I told you that I wanted you to share in the estate. I know my father could drive people over the edge. I'm doing this because I'm sorry for you. Now here are the figures.'

For the next fifteen minutes, Lillian pulled balance sheets out of the file. 'Allowing for taxes and then interest made on the remainder, your share would now be five million dollars.'

'And this house,' Cynthia interjected. Bewildered, she realized that with each passing moment Lillian and Ned were becoming more visibly relaxed. They were both smiling.

'Oh, not the house,' Lillian protested. 'There'd be too much gossip. We'll have the house appraised, and I'll pay you the value of it. Remember, Cynthia, I'm being very generous. My father toyed with people's lives. He was cruel. If you hadn't killed him, someone else would have. That's why I'm doing this.'

'You're doing it because you don't want to sit in a courtroom and take a chance on being convicted of murder, that's why you're doing it.' Oh God. Cynthia thought. It's no use. If I can't get her to admit it, it's all over. By tomorrow Lillian and Ned would have a chance to check on Alvirah. 'You can have the house,' she said. 'Don't pay me for it. Just give me the satisfaction of hearing the truth. Admit that I had nothing to do with your father's murder.'

Lillian glanced at Ned, then at the clock. 'I think at this time we should honor that request.' She began to laugh. 'Cynthia, I *am* like my father. I enjoy toying with people. My father *did* phone to tell me about the change in his will. I could live with Dartmouth getting half the estate but not you. He told me you were coming up – and the rest was easy. My mother was a wonderful woman. She was only too happy to verify that I was in New York with her that evening. Ned was delighted to get a great deal of money for giving you a boat ride. You're smart, Cynthia. Smarter than the district attorney's office. Smarter than that dumb lawyer you had.'

Let the recorder be working, Cynthia prayed. Let it be working. 'And smart enough to find the witness who could verify my story,' she added.

Lillian and Ned burst into laughter. 'What witness?' Ned asked.

'Get out,' Lillian told her. 'Get out this minute. And don't come back.'

Jeff Knight drove swiftly along Route 6, trying to read signs through the torrential rain that was slashing the windshield. Exit 8. He was coming up to it. The producer of the ten o'clock news had been unexpectedly decent. Of course there was a reason. 'Go ahead. If Cynthia Lathem is on the Cape and thinks she has a lead on her stepfather's death, you've got a great story breaking.'

Jeff wasn't interested in the great story. His only concern was Cynthia. Now he gripped the steering wheel with his long, strong fingers. He had managed to get her address as well as her phone number from her parole officer. He'd spend a lot of summers on the Cape. That was why it had been so frustrating when he tried to prove Cynthia's story about stopping at the hamburger stand and got nowhere. But he'd always stayed in Eastham, some fifty miles from Cotuit.

Exit 8. He turned onto Union Street, drove to Route 6A. A couple of miles more. Why did he have this sense of impending doom? If Cynthia had a real lead that could help her, she could be in danger.

He had to slam on his brakes when he reached Nobscusset Road. Another car ignoring the stop sign raced from Nobscusset across Route 6A. Damn fool, Jeff thought as he turned toward the Bay. He realized that the whole area was in darkness. A power failure. He reached the dead end, turned left. The cottage had to be on this winding lane. Number six. He drove slowly, trying to read the numbers as his headlights shone on the mailboxes. Twelve. Eight. Six.

Jeff pulled into the driveway, threw open the door and ran through the pelting rain toward the cottage. He held his finger on the bell, then realized that

128

because of the power failure it did not work. He pounded on the door several times. There was no answer. Cynthia wasn't home.

He started to walk down the steps, then a sudden, reasoning fear made him go back, pound again on the door, then turn the knob. It twisted in his hand. He pushed it open. 'Cynthia,' he started to call, then gasped as the odor of gas rushed at him. He could hear the hissing of the jet from the fireplace. Rushing to turn it off, he tripped over the prone figure of Alvirah.

Willy moved restlessly in the back seat of Cynthia's car. She'd been in that house for more than an hour now. The guy who'd come later had been there 15 minutes. Willy wasn't sure what to do. Alvirah really hadn't given specific instructions. She just wanted him to be around to make sure Cynthia didn't leave the house with anyone.

As he debated, he heard the screeching sound of sirens. Police cars. The sirens got closer. Astonished, Willy watched as they turned into the long driveway of the Richards' estate and thundered toward him. Policemen rushed from the squad cars, raced up the steps and pounded on the door.

A moment later a sedan pulled into the driveway and stopped behind the squad cars. As Willy watched, a big fellow in a trench coat leaped out of it and took the steps to the porch two at a time. Willy climbed awkwardly to his feet then and hoisted himself to the driveway.

He was in time to grab Alvirah as she staggered from the back of the sedan. Even in the dark he could see the welt on her forehead. 'Honey, what happened?'

'I'll tell you later. Get me inside. I don't want to miss this.'

In the study of the late Stuart Richards, Alvirah experienced her finest hour. Pointing her finger at Ned, in her most vibrant tones, she pronounced, 'He held a gun to me. He turned on the gas jet. He smashed my head against the fireplace. And told me that Lillian Richards paid him three million dollars to set up Cynthia as the murderer.'

Cynthia stared at her stepsister. 'And unless the batteries in Alvirah's recorder are dead, I have both of them on record admitting their guilt.'

The next morning Willy fixed a late breakfast and served it on the deck. The storm had ended and once again the sky was joyously blue. Seagulls swooped down to feast on surfacing fish. The Bay was tranquil, and children were making castles in the damp sand at the water's edge.

Alvirah, not that much worse for her experience, had finished her article and phoned it in to Charley Evans. Charley had promised her the most ornate silver starburst pin that money could buy, one with a microphone so sensitive it could pick up a mouse sneezing in the next room.

Now as she munched a chocolate-covered doughnut and sipped coffee, she said, 'Oh, here comes Jeff. What a shame he had to drive back to Boston last night, but wasn't he wonderful telling the story on the news this morning? Buhlieve me, he'll go places with the networks.'

'That guy saved your life, honey,' Willy said. 'He's aces high with me. I can't believe I was curled up in that car like a jack-in-the-box when you had your head in a gas jet.'

They watched as Jeff got out of the car and Cynthia rushed down the walk into his arms.

Alvirah pushed her chair back. 'I'll run over and say

hello. It's a treat to see how they look at each other. They're so in love.'

Willy placed a gentle but firm hand on her shoulder. 'Alvirah, honey,' he begged, 'just this once, for five minutes, mind your own business.'

The Body in the Closet

If on that August evening, Alvirah Meehan had known what was waiting for her at her fancy new apartment on Central Park South, she would never have gotten off the plane. As it was, there was absolutely no hint of foreboding in her usually keen psyche as the plane circled for a landing.

Even though she and Willy had been bitten by the travel bug after they won the lottery, Alvirah was always glad to get back to New York. There was something heartwarming about seeing the skyscrapers silhouetted against the clouds and the lights of the bridge that spanned the East River.

Willy patted her hand and Alvirah turned to him with an affectionate smile. He looked grand, she thought, in his new blue linen jacket that matched the color of his eyes. With those eyes and his thick head of white hair, Willy was a double for Tip O'Neill, no mistake about it.

Alvirah smoothed her russet-brown hair, recently tinted and styled by Dale of London. Dale had marveled to hear that Alvirah was sixty. 'You're funning me,' he gasped.

Gleaming on her lapel was her sunburst pin with its hidden microphone. Alvirah recorded conversations she could use for her feature articles in the *New York Globe*. 'The trip was wonderful,' she observed now to Willy, 'but it wasn't an adventure I could write about.

The most exciting thing was when the Queen stopped in for tea at the Stafford Court Hotel and the manager's cat attacked her corgis.'

'I'm just glad we had a nice, calm vacation,' Willy said. 'I can't take much more of you almost getting killed solving crimes.'

The British Airways attendant was walking down the aisle of the first-class cabin checking that seat belts were fastened. 'I certainly enjoyed talking with you,' she told them. Willy had explained that he'd been a plumber and Alvirah a cleaning woman until they won the forty-million-dollar lottery. 'My goodness,' she said now to Alvirah. 'I just can't believe you were ever a char.'

In a mercifully short time after landing they were in a cab, their matching Vuitton luggage stacked in the trunk. As usual, New York in August was hot, sticky and sultry. The cab was a steam box and Alvirah thought longingly ahead to her new apartment on Central Park South, which of course would be wonderfully cool. They still kept their old three-room flat in Flushing where they'd lived for 30 years before the lottery changed their lives. As Willy pointed out, you never knew if someday New York would go broke and tell the lottery winners to take a flying leap for the rest of the checks. They kept the flat and a nest egg in the Citizens of Flushing Bank just in case.

When the cab pulled up to the apartment building the doorman, in red and gold with a massive black fur hat, opened the door for them. 'You must be melting,' Alvirah said. 'You'd think they wouldn't bother dressing you up until they finished the renovations.'

The building was undergoing a total overhaul. When they had bought the apartment in the spring, the real estate agent had assured them that the refurbishing would be completed in a matter of weeks. It was clear from the scaffolding in the lobby that he had been wildly optimistic.

At the bank of elevators they were joined by another couple, a tall, fiftyish man and a slender woman in a white silk evening suit with an expression that reminded Alvirah of someone who has opened a refrigerator and encountered the odor of eggs gone bad. I know them, Alvirah thought and began ruffling through her prodigious memory. He was Carleton Rumson, the legendary Broadway producer, and she was his wife, Victoria, a sometime actress who had been a Miss America runner-up thirty years ago.

'Mr. Rumson!' With a smile that softened her somewhat jutting jaw, Alvirah reached out her hand. 'I'm Alvirah Meehan. We met at the Cypress Point Spa in Pebble Beach. What a nice surprise! This is my husband, Willy. Do you live here?'

Rumson's smile came and went. 'We keep an apartment for convenience.' He nodded to Willy, then grudgingly introduced his wife. The elevator door opened as Victoria Rumson acknowledged them with the flicker of an eyelid. What a cold fish, Alvirah thought, taking in the perfect but haughty profile, the pale-blonde hair pulled back into a chignon. Long years of reading *People, US*, the *National Enquirer* and gossip columns had resulted in Alvirah's brain becoming the repository of an awesome amount of information about the rich and famous.

They had just stopped at the thirty-fourth floor as Alvirah remembered her Rumson tidbits. Rumson was famous for his wandering eye. His wife's ability to overlook his indiscretions had earned her the nickname of 'see-no-evil-Vicky'.

'Mr. Rumson,' Alvirah said, 'Willy's nephew, Brian McCormack, is a wonderful playwright. He's just finished his second play. I'd love to have you read it.'

Rumson looked annoyed. 'My office is listed in the phone book,' he said.

'Brian's first play is running Off-Broadway right now,' Alvirah persisted. 'One of the critics said he's a young Neil Simon.'

'Come on, honey,' Willy urged. 'You're holding up these folks.'

Unexpectedly the glacier look melted from Victoria Rumson's face. 'Darling,' she said, 'I've heard about Brian McCormack. Why don't you read the play here? It will only get buried if you have it sent to your office.'

'That's real nice of you, Victoria,' Alvirah said heartily. 'You'll have it tomorrow.'

As they walked from the elevator to their apartment, Willy asked, 'Honey, don't you think you were being a little pushy?'

'Absolutely not,' Alvirah said. 'Nothing ventured, nothing gained. Anything I can do to help Brian's career is A-okay with me.'

Their apartment commanded a sweeping view of Central Park. Alvirah never stepped into it without thinking that not so long ago she had considered her Thursday cleaning job, Mrs. Chester Lollop's house in Little Neck, a miniature palace. Boy, had her eyes opened these last few years!

They'd bought the apartment completely furnished from a stockbroker who'd been indicted for insider trading. He had just had it done by an interior designer who, he assured them, was the absolute rage of Manhattan. Secretly Alvirah now had serious doubts about that. The living room, dining room and kitchen were stark white. There were low white sofas that she had to hoist herself out of, thick white carpeting that showed every speck of dirt, white counters and cabinets and marble, and appliances that reminded her of all the tubs and sinks and toilets she'd ever tried to scrub free of rust.

There was a large printed sign taped to the door leading to the terrace.

A building inspection has revealed that this is one of a small number of apartments in which a serious structural weakness has been found in the guardrailing and the panels of the terrace. Your terrace is safe for normal use, but do not lean on the guardrail or permit others to do so. Repairs will be completed as rapidly as possible.

Alvirah shrugged. 'Well, I certainly have brains enough not to lean on any guardrail, safe or not.'

Willy smiled sheepishly. He was scared silly of heights and never had set foot on the terrace. As he'd said when they bought the apartment, 'You love a terrace. I love terra firma.'

Willy went into the kitchen to put the kettle on. Alvirah opened the terrace door and stepped outside. The sultry air was a hot wave against her face but she didn't care. There was something about standing out here, looking across the park at the festive glow from the decorated trees around the Tavern on the Green, the ribbons of headlights from the cars, the glimpses of horse-drawn carriages in the distance.

Oh, it's good to be back, she thought again as she went inside and surveyed the living room, her expert eye observing the degree of activity of the weekly cleaning service that should have been in yesterday. She was surprised to see fingerprints smeared across the glass cocktail table. Automatically she reached for a handkerchief and vigorously rubbed them away. Then she noticed that the tieback on the drapery next to the terrace door was missing. Hope it didn't end up in the vacuum, she thought. At least *I* was a good cleaning woman. She remembered what the British Airways attendant had said. Or a good char, whatever that is.

'Hey, Alvirah,' Willy called. 'Did Brian leave a note? Looks like he might have been expecting someone.'

Brian, Willy's nephew, was the only child of his oldest sister Madelaine. Six of Willy's seven sisters had gone into the convent. Madelaine had married in her forties and produced a change-of-life baby, Brian, who was now twenty-six years old. He had been raised in Nebraska, written plays for a repertory company out there and came to New York after Madelaine's death two years ago. All of Alvirah's untapped maternal instincts were released by Brian with his thin, intense face, unruly sandy hair and shy smile. As she often told Willy, 'If I'd carried him inside me for nine months, I couldn't love him more.'

When they'd left for England in June, Brian was finishing the first draft of his new play and had been glad to accept their offer of a key to the Central Park apartment. 'It's a heck of a lot easier to write there than in my place,' was his grateful comment. He lived in a walk-up in the East Village surrounded by noisy families.

Alvirah went into the kitchen. She raised her eyes. Two champagne glasses and a bottle of champagne in a wine cooler were on a silver tray. The champagne, a gift from the broker who'd handled the apartment sale, was standing in the wine cooler half-filled with water. The broker had several times informed them that the champagne cost five hundred dollars a bottle and was what the Queen of England enjoyed sipping.

Willy looked troubled. 'That's the stuff that's so crazy expensive, isn't it? No way Brian would help himself to that. There's something funny going on.' Alvirah opened her mouth to reassure him, then closed it. There *was* something funny going on and her antenna told her trouble was brewing.

The chimes rang. An apologetic porter was at the

137

door with their bags. 'Sorry to be so long, Mr. Meehan. Since the remodeling began, so many residents are using the service elevator that the staff has to stand in line for it.' At Willy's request, he deposited the bags in the bedroom, then departed smiling, his palm closing over a five-dollar bill.

Willy and Alvirah shared a pot of tea in the kitchen. Willy kept staring at the champagne. 'I'm gonna call Brian,' he decided.

'He'll still be at the theater,' Alvirah said, closed her eyes, concentrated and gave him the telephone number of the box office.

Willy dialed, listened, then hung up. 'There's a recorder on,' he said flatly. 'Brian's play closed. They talk about how to get refunds.'

'The poor kid,' Alvirah breathed. 'Try his apartment.'

'Only the answering machine,' he told her a moment later. 'I'll leave a message for him.'

Alvirah suddenly realized how weary she was. As she collected teacups she reminded herself that it was five A.M., English time, so she had a right to feel as though all her bones were aching. She put the teacups in the dishwasher, hesitated, then rinsed out the unused champagne glasses and put them in the dishwasher too. Her friend Baroness Min von Schreiber – who owned the Cypress Point Spa where Alvirah had gone to be made over after she won the lottery – had told her that expensive wines should not be left standing. With a damp sponge, she gave a vigorous rub to the unopened bottle. Turning the lights out behind her, she went into the bedroom.

Willy had begun to unpack. Alvirah liked the bedroom. It had been furnished for the bachelor stockbroker with a king-sized bed, a triple dresser, night tables large enough to hold books, reading glasses and mineral ice for Alvirah's rheumatic knees, and comfortable easy chairs by the window. However, the decor convinced her that the trendy interior designer must have been weaned on bleach. White spread. White drapes. White carpet.

The porter had left Alvirah's garment bag spread out across the bed. She unlocked it and began to remove the suits and dresses. Baroness von Schreiber was always pleading with her not to go shopping on her own. 'Alvirah,' Min would argue, 'you are natural prey for saleswomen who have been ordered to unload the buyer's mistakes. They sense your approach even while you're still in the elevator. I'm in New York enough. You come to the Spa several times a year. I will shop with you.'

Alvirah wondered if Min would approve of the orange and pink plaid that the saleswoman in Harrod's had raved over. She was sure she wouldn't.

Her arms filled with clothing, she opened the door of the closet, glanced down and let out a shriek. Lying on the carpeted floor between the rows of Alvirah's size-ten extra-wide designer shoes, green eyes staring up, crinkly blonde hair flowing around her face, tongue slightly protruding and the missing drapery tieback around her neck, was the body of a slender young woman.

'Blessed Mother,' Alvirah moaned as the clothes fell from her arms.

'What's the matter, honey?' Willy demanded, rushing to her side. 'Oh, my God,' he breathed. 'Who the hell is that?'

'It's . . . it's . . . you know. The actress. The one who had the lead in Brian's play. The one Brian is so crazy about.' Alvirah squeezed her eyes shut, glad to free herself from the glazed expression on the face of the body at her feet. 'Fiona, that's who it is. Fiona Winters.'

139

Willy's arm firmly around her, Alvirah walked to the low couch in the living room, the one that made her knees feel as though they were going to stab her chin. As he dialed 911, she forced her head to clear. It doesn't take a lot of brains to know that this could look very bad for Brian. She thought, I've got to get my thinking cap on and remember everything I can about that girl. She was so nasty to Brian. Did they have a fight?

Willy crossed the room, sat beside her and reached for her hand. 'It's going to be all right, honey,' he said soothingly. 'The cops will be here in a few minutes.'

'Call Brian again,' Alvirah told him.

'Good idea.' Willy dialed quickly. 'Just that darn machine. I'll leave another message. Try to rest.'

Alvirah nodded, closed her eyes and immediately turned her thoughts to the night last April when Brian's play opened.

The theater was crowded. Brian arranged for them to have front-row-center seats and Alvirah wore her new silver and black sequin dress. The play, *Falling Bridges*, was set in Nebraska and was about a family reunion. Fiona Winters played the socialite who is bored with her unsophisticated in-laws and Alvirah had to admit she was very believable. Alvirah liked the girl who played the second lead much better. Emmy Laker had bright-red hair, blue eyes and portrayed a funny but wistful character to perfection.

The performances brought a standing ovation, and Alvirah's heart swelled with pride when the cries of 'Author! Author!' brought Brian to the stage. When he was handed a bouquet and leaned over to the footlights to give it to Alvirah she started to cry.

The opening-night party was in the upstairs room of Gallagher's Steak House. Brian kept the seats on either side of him for Alvirah and Fiona Winters. Willy and Emmy Laker sat opposite. It didn't take Alvirah long to get the lay of the land. Brian hovered over Fiona Winters like a lovesick idiot. Winters had a way of putting him down and letting them know about her high-class background, saying, 'The family was appalled when after Foxcroft I decided to go into the theater.' She then proceeded to tell Willy and Brian, who were thoroughly enjoying sliced-steak sandwiches with Gallagher's special fries, that they were likely candidates for heart attacks. Personally, she never ate meat.

She took pot shots at all of us, Alvirah recalled. She asked me if I missed cleaning houses. She told me Brian should learn to dress and with our income she's surprised we don't help him out. She jumped on that sweet girl, Emmy Laker, when Emmy said Brian had better things to think about than his wardrobe.

On the way home she and Willy had solemnly agreed that Brian had a lot of growing-up to do if he didn't see what a mean type Fiona was. 'I'd like to see him together with Emmy Laker,' Willy had announced. 'If he had the brains he was born with he'd know that she's crazy about him. And that Fiona has been around a lot. She must have eight years on Brian.'

The bell rang vigorously. Mother-in-heaven, Alvirah thought. I wish I'd had a chance to talk to Brian.

The next hours passed in a blur. As her head cleared a bit, Alvirah realized that she was able to separate the different kinds of law-enforcement people who invaded the apartment. The first were the policemen in uniform. Then detectives, photographers, the medical examiners. She and Willy sat together silently observing them all.

Officials from the Central Park South Towers office

came too. 'We hope there will be no unfortunate publicity,' the resident manager said. 'This is not the Trump Organization.'

Their original statement had been taken by the first two cops. At three A.M., the door from the bedroom opened. 'Don't look, honey,' Willy said. But Alvirah could not keep her eyes away from the stretcher that two somber-faced attendants carried out. At least the body of Fiona Winters was covered. God rest her, Alvirah prayed, seeing again the tousled blonde hair and the pouty lips. Alvirah thought, she was not a nice person but she certainly didn't deserve to die.

Someone came to sit opposite them, a long-legged fortyish man who introduced himself as Detective Rooney. 'I read your articles in the *Globe*, Mrs. Meehan,' he told Alvirah, 'and thoroughly enjoyed them.'

Willy smiled appreciatively but Alvirah wasn't fooled. She knew Detective Rooney was buttering her up to make her confide in him. Her mind was racing trying to figure out ways to protect Brian. Automatically she reached up and switched on the microphone in her sunburst pin. Later she wanted to be able to go over everything that was said.

Detective Rooney consulted his notes. 'According to your earlier statement, you've just returned from a vacation abroad and arrived here around ten P.M. You found the victim, Fiona Winters, a short time later. You recognized Miss Winters because she played the lead in your nephew Brian McCormack's play.'

Alvirah nodded. She noticed that Willy was about to speak and laid a warning hand on his arm. 'That's right.'

'From what I understand, you only met Miss Winters once,' Detective Rooney said. 'How do you suppose she ended up in your closet?'

'I have no idea,' Alvirah said.

142

'Who had a key to this apartment?'

Again Willy's lips pursed. This time Alvirah pinched his arm. 'Keys to this apartment,' she said thoughtfully. 'Now let me see. The One-Two-Three Cleaning Service has a key. Well, they don't really *have* a key. They pick one up at the desk and leave it there when they finish. My friend, Maude, has a key. She came in Mother's Day weekend to go out with her son and his wife to Windows on the World. They have a cat and she's allergic to cats so she slept on our couch. Then Willy's sister, Sister Patricia, has a key. Then . . . '

'Does your nephew, Brian McCormack, have a key, Mrs. Meehan?' Detective Rooney interrupted.

Alvirah bit her lip.

'Brian McCormack has a key.' This time Detective Rooney raised his voice slightly. 'According to the concierge, he's been using this apartment frequently in your absence. Incidentally, although it's impossible to be totally accurate before an autopsy, the Medical Examiner estimates the time of death between eleven A.M. and three P.M. yesterday.' Detective Rooney's tone became speculative. 'It will be interesting to know where Brian McCormack was during that time frame.'

They were told that before they could use the apartment, the investigating team would have to dust it for fingerprints and vacuum it for clues. 'The apartment is as you found it?' Detective Rooney asked.

'Except,' Willy began.

'Except that we made a pot of tea,' Alvirah interrupted. I can always tell them about the wineglasses and the champagne but I can't untell them, she thought. That detective is going to find out that Brian was crazy about Fiona Winters and decide it was a crime of passion. Then he'll make everything fit that theory.

143

Detective Rooney closed his notebook. 'I understand the management has a furnished apartment you can use tonight,' he said.

Fifteen minutes later, Alvirah was in bed gratefully hunched against an already dozing Willy. Tired as she was, it was hard to relax in a strange bed. She thought this could look very bad for Brian. There has to be an explanation. Brian wouldn't help himself to that five-hundred-dollar bottle of champagne and he certainly wouldn't kill Fiona Winters. But how did she end up in my closet?

Despite the late bedtime, Alvirah and Willy were up at seven A.M. As their mutual shock over the body in the closet wore off, they began to worry about Brian. 'No use fretting about Brian,' Alvirah said with a heartiness she did not feel. 'When we talk to him, I'm sure everything will be cleared up. Let's see if we can get back into our place.'

They dressed quickly and hurried out. Carleton Rumson was standing at the elevators. His pink complexion was sallow. Dark pouches under his eyes added ten years to his appearance. Automatically, Alvirah reached up and switched on the microphone in her pin.

'Mr. Rumson?' she asked, 'did you hear the terrible news about the murder in our apartment?'

Rumson pressed vigorously for the elevator. 'As a matter of fact, yes. Friends in the building phoned us. Terrible for the young lady, terrible for you.'

The elevator arrived. After they got in, Rumson said, 'Mrs. Meehan, my wife reminded me about your nephew's play. We're leaving for Mexico tomorrow morning. I'd very much like to read it today.'

Alvirah's jaw dropped. 'Oh, that's wonderful of your wife to keep after you about it. We'll make sure to get it up to you.'

When she and Willy got out at their floor, she said, 'This could be Brian's big break. Provided that . . .' she said, stopping in mid-sentence.

A policeman was on guard at the door of their apartment. Inside, every surface was smeared because the investigators had dusted for fingerprints. And seated across from Detective Rooney, looking bewildered and forlorn, was Brian. He jumped up. 'Aunt Alvirah, I'm sorry. This is awful for you.'

To Alvirah he looked about ten years old. His T-shirt and khaki shorts were rumpled; had he dressed to escape a burning building he could not have looked more disheveled.

Alvirah brushed back the sandy hair that fell over Brian's forehead as Willy grasped his hand. 'You okay?' Willy asked.

Brian managed a troubled smile. 'I guess so.'

Detective Rooney interrupted. 'Mr. McCormack just arrived and I was about to inform him that he is a suspect in the death of Fiona Winters and has the right to counsel.'

'Are you kidding?' Brian asked, his tone incredulous.

'I assure you, I'm not kidding.' Detective Rooney pulled a paper from his breast pocket. He read Brian his Miranda rights, then handed it to Brian. 'Please let me know if you understand its meaning.'

Rooney looked at Alvirah and Willy. 'Our people are through. You can stay in the apartment now. I'll take Mr. McCormack's statement at headquarters.'

'Brian, don't say one word until we get you a lawyer,' Willy ordered.

Brian shook his head. 'Uncle Willy, I have nothing to hide. I don't need a lawyer.'

Alvirah kissed Brian. 'Come right back here when you're finished,' she told him.

The condition of the apartment gave her something to do. She dispatched Willy with a long shopping list, warning him to take the service elevator to avoid reporters.

As she vacuumed and scrubbed and mopped and dusted, Alvirah realized with increasing dread that cops don't give a Miranda warning unless they have a pretty good reason for suspecting someone's guilt.

The hardest job was to vacuum the closet. It was as though she could see again the wide-open eyes of Fiona Winters staring up at her. That thought led her to another one. If Fiona had been strangled by someone who came up behind her, she wouldn't have been found lying on her back facing upward.

Alvirah dropped the handle of the vacuum. She thought about those fingerprints on the cocktail table. If Fiona Winters had been sitting on the couch, maybe leaning forward a little, and her killer walked behind it, slipped the tieback around her neck and twisted it, wouldn't her hand have pulled back like that? 'Saints and angels,' Alvirah whispered, 'I bet I destroyed evidence.'

The phone rang just as she was fastening her pin to her lapel. It was Baroness Min von Schreiber calling from the Cypress Point Spa in Pebble Beach, California. Min had just heard the news. 'Whatever was that dreadful girl thinking about getting herself killed in your closet?' Min demanded.

'Buhlieve me, Min,' Alvirah said. 'I met her once when we went to see Brian's play. The cops are questioning Brian right now. I'm worried sick. They think he killed her.'

'You're wrong, Alvirah,' Min said. 'You met Fiona Winters out here at the spa.'

'Never,' Alvirah said positively. 'She was the kind who got on your nerves so much you'd never forget her.'

146

There was a pause. 'I am thinking,' Min announced. 'You're right. She came another week with someone and they spent the weekend in the cottage. They even had their meals served there. It was that hotshot producer she was trying to snare. Carleton Rumson. You remember him, Alvirah. You met him another time when he was here alone.'

At noon when Carleton Rumson returned the reporters swarmed around him and besieged him with questions.

'Yes, Miss Winters appeared in several of my productions. No, I had no idea she was visiting in this building. If you'll excuse me now, I must . . .'

He managed to shoulder his way through the crowd. Had he touched anything in that apartment yesterday, he wondered. Had he left fingerprints? The thought sent cold chills through his body.

Alvirah went into the living room and out on to the terrace. Willy gets so nervous if I even step out here, she thought, and that's crazy. The only thing to be careful about is leaning on the railing.

The humidity was near saturation point. Not a leaf in the park stirred. Even so Alvirah sighed with pleasure. How can anyone who was born in New York stay away from it for long, she wondered.

Willy brought in the newspapers with the groceries. One headline screeched 'Murder on Central Park South'; another, 'Lottery Winner Finds Body'. Alvirah carefully read the lurid accounts. 'I didn't scream and faint,' she scoffed. 'Where'd they get that idea?'

'According to the *Post*, you were hanging up the fabulous new wardrobe you bought in London,' Willy told her.

'Fabulous new wardrobe! The only expensive thing

147

I bought was that orange and pink plaid suit – and I know Min is going to make me give it away.'

There were columns of background material on Fiona Winters: the break with her socialite family when she went into acting; her uneven career; she'd won a Tony but was notoriously difficult to work with, which had cost her a number of plum roles; her break with playwright Brian McCormack when she abruptly walked out of his play *Falling Bridges*, forcing it to close.

'Motive,' Alvirah said flatly. 'By tomorrow they'll be trying this case in the papers and Brian will be found guilty.'

At twelve-thirty P.M. Brian returned. Alvirah took one look at his ashen face and ordered him to sit down. 'I'll make a pot of tea and fix you a hamburger,' she said. 'You look like you're going to keel over.'

'I think a shot of Scotch would do a lot more good than tea,' Willy observed.

Brian managed a wan smile. 'I think you're right, Uncle Willy.' Over hamburgers and French fries he told them what had happened. 'I swear I didn't think they'd let me go. They're sure I killed her.'

'Is it okay if I turn on my microphone?' Alvirah asked. She fiddled with the sunburst pin, touching the microphone switch. 'Now, tell us exactly what you told them.'

Brian frowned. 'A lot about my personal relationship with Fiona. I was sick of her lousy disposition and I was falling in love with Emmy. I told them that when she quit the play it was the last straw.'

'But how did she get in my closet?' Alvirah asked. 'You must have been the one who let her into the apartment.'

'I did. I've been working here a lot. You were coming back so I cleared my stuff out day before yesterday.

148

Then yesterday Fiona phoned and said she was back in New York and would be right over to see me. By mistake I'd left my notes for my final draft here with my backup copy. I told her not to waste time, that I was heading here to get my notes and then was going to be at the typewriter all day and wouldn't answer my door. I found her parked downstairs in the lobby, and rather than make a scene I let her come up.'

'What did she want?' Alvirah and Willy both asked.

'Nothing much. Just the lead in *Nebraska Nights*.'

'After walking out on the other one!'

'She put on the performance of her life. Begged me to forgive her. Said she'd been a fool to leave *Falling Bridges*. Her role in the film was ending up on the cutting-room floor and the bad publicity about dumping the play had hurt her. Wanted to know if *Nebraska Nights* was finished yet. I'm human. I bragged about it. Told her it might take time to find the right producer but when I did it was going to be a big hit.'

'Had she ever read it?' Alvirah asked.

Brian studied the tea leaves in his cup. 'These don't make for much of a fortune,' he commented. 'She knew the story line and that there's a fantastic lead role for an actress.'

'You certainly didn't promise it to her?' Alvirah exclaimed.

Brian shook his head. 'Aunt Alvirah, I know she played me for a fool, but I couldn't believe she thought I was that much of a fool. She asked me to make a deal. She had access to one of the biggest producers on Broadway. If she could get it to him and he took it, she wanted to play Diane – I mean Beth.'

'Who's that?' Willy asked.

'The name of the leading character. I changed it on the final draft last night. I told Fiona she had to be kidding, but if she could pull that off I might consider it.

Then I got my notes and tried to get her out of here. She said she had an audition at Lincoln Center and wanted to stay for an hour or so. She wouldn't budge. I finally decided there probably wasn't any harm in leaving her so I could get work done. The last time I saw her was just about noon and she was sitting on that couch.'

'Did she know you had a copy of the new play here?' Alvirah asked.

'Sure. I took it out of the drawer of the table when I was getting the notes.' He pointed toward the foyer. 'It's in that drawer now.'

Alvirah got up, walked quickly to the foyer and pulled open the drawer. As she had expected, it was empty.

Emmy Laker sat motionless on the oversized club chair in her West Side studio apartment. Ever since she had heard about Fiona's death on the seven o'clock news she'd been trying to reach Brian. Had he been arrested? Oh God, not Brian, she thought. What should I do? Despairingly, she looked at the luggage in the corner of the room. Fiona's luggage.

Yesterday morning the bell had rung at eight-thirty. When she opened the door, Fiona swept in. 'How can you stand living in a walk-up?' she'd demanded. 'Thank God, some kid was making a delivery and carried these up.' She'd dropped her suitcases and reached for a cigarette. 'I came in on the red-eye. What a mistake to take that job. I told the director off and he fired me. I've been trying to reach Brian. Do you know where he is?'

At the memory, rage swelled in Emmy. 'I hated her,' she said aloud. As though she were still across the room she could see Fiona, her blonde hair tousled, her body-hugging jumpsuit showing off every inch of

150

that perfect figure, her cat's eyes insolent and confident.

She was so sure that even after the way she treated Brian she could still walk back into his life, Emmy thought, remembering all the months when she had agonized at the sight of Brian with Fiona. Would that have happened again? Yesterday she had thought it possible.

Fiona kept phoning Brian until she reached him. When she hung up she said, 'Mind if I leave my bags here? Brian's on his way to the cleaning woman's fancy pad. I'll head him off.' Then she'd shrugged. 'He's so damn provincial, but it's amazing how many people on the West Coast know about him. I must say from what I heard about *Nebraska Nights* it has all the earmarks of a hit – and I intend to play the lead.'

Now Emmy got up. Her body felt stiff and achy. The old window-unit air conditioner was rattling and wheezing but the room was still hot and humid. A cool shower and a cup of coffee, she thought. Maybe that will clear my head. She wanted to see Brian. She wanted to put her arms around him. I'm not sorry Fiona's dead, she admitted, but oh, Brian, how did you expect to get away with it?

She had just dressed in a T-shirt and cotton skirt and twisted her long bright-red hair in a chignon when the buzzer downstairs ran. When she answered it was to hear Detective Rooney announce that he was on his way up.

'This is starting to make sense,' Alvirah said. 'Brian, is there anything you left out? For instance, did you put the bottle of that fit-for-a-queen champagne in the silver bucket yesterday?'

Brian looked bewildered. 'Why would I do that?'

'I didn't think you would. Oh boy, what a story.

Fiona didn't hang around because she had an audition. It's my bet she phoned Carleton Rumson and invited him down here. That's why the wineglasses and champagne were out. She gave him the script and then, who knows why, they got into a fight. I've got my thinking cap on,' she told Brian. 'I want you to go home and get your final version of the play. I talked to Carleton Rumson, the producer, about it and he wants to see it today.'

'Carleton Rumson!' Brian exclaimed. 'He's the biggest on Broadway and the hardest to reach. You must be a magician!'

'I'll tell you about it later. He and his wife are going away, so let's strike while the iron is hot.'

Brian glanced at the phone. 'I should call Emmy. She certainly must have heard about Fiona by now.' He dialed the number and waited. His tone disappointed, he said, 'I guess she's out.'

Emmy was sure it was Brian phoning but made no move to pick up the receiver. The thin, somber-faced man sitting across from her had just asked her to describe in detail what she had done the previous day. Emmy chose her words carefully. 'I left here about eleven A.M. and I went jogging. I got back about one-thirty P.M. and stayed in the rest of the day.'

'Alone?'

'Yes.'

'Did you see Fiona Winters yesterday?' Emmy's eyes slid over to the corner where the luggage was piled. 'I . . . ' She stopped.

'Miss Laker, I think I should warn you that it will be in your best interest to be completely truthful.' Detective Rooney consulted his notes. 'Fiona Winters came in on a flight from Los Angeles, arriving at approximately seven-thirty A.M. She took a cab to this building. A delivery boy who recognized her assisted her with her luggage. She told him that you would not be glad to see her because you're after her boyfriend. When Miss Winters left, you followed her. A doorman on Central Park South recognized you. You sat on a park bench across the street watching the building for nearly two hours and then entered it by the delivery door, which had been propped open by the painters.' Detective Rooney leaned forward. His tone became confidential. 'You went up to the Meehans' apartment, didn't you? Was Miss Winters already dead?'

Emmy stared at her hands. Brian always teased her about how small they were. 'But strong,' he'd laugh when they'd arm-wrestle. Brian. No matter what she said she would hurt him. She looked up at Detective Rooney. 'I want to talk to a lawyer.'

Rooney got up. 'That is, of course, your privilege. I would like to remind you that if Brian McCormack murdered his ex-lover, you can become an accessory after the fact by concealing evidence. And I assure you, you wouldn't do him any good. We expect an indictment from the grand jury.'

When Brian reached his apartment, there was a message on the recorder from Emmy. 'Call me, Brian. Please.' Brian's fingers worked with frantic haste as he dialed her number.

She whispered, 'Hello.'

'Emmy, what's the matter? I tried you before but you were out.'

'I was here. A detective came. Brian, I have to see you.'

'Take a cab to my aunt's place. I'm on my way back there.'

'I want to talk to you alone. It's about Fiona. She was here yesterday. I followed her over to the apartment.'

Brian felt his mouth go dry. 'Don't say anything else on the phone.'

At four P.M., the bell rang insistently. Alvirah jumped up. 'Brian forgot his key,' she told Willy. 'I noticed it on the foyer table.'

But it was Carleton Rumson standing at the door. 'Mrs. Meehan, please forgive the intrusion.' With that, he stepped inside.

'I mentioned to one of my assistants that I was going to look at your nephew's play. Apparently he saw his first one and thought it was very good. In fact he had urged me to see it.' Rumson walked into the living room and sat down. Nervously he drummed his fingers on the cocktail table.

'Can I get you a drink?' Willy asked. 'Or maybe a beer?'

'Oh, Willy,' Alvirah said. 'I'm just sure that Mr. Rumson only drinks fine champagne. Maybe I read that in *People*.'

'As a matter of fact, it's true, but not right now, thank you.' Rumson's expression was affable enough, but Alvirah noticed that a pulse was jumping in his throat. 'Where can I reach your nephew?'

'He'll be here soon. I'll call the minute he gets in.'

'I'm a fast read. If you would send the script up, he and I could get together an hour or so later.'

When Rumson left, Alvirah asked Willy, 'What are you thinking?'

'That for a hotshot producer, he's some nervous wreck. I hate people tapping their fingers on tabletops. Gives me the jitters.'

'It was giving him the jitters not to have the chance to do it here.' Alvirah smiled at Willy mysteriously.

Less than a minute later the bell rang again. Alvirah hurried to the door. Emmy Laker was there, wisps of red hair slipping from the chignon, dark glasses covering half her face, the T-shirt clinging to her slender body, the cotton skirt a colorful whirl. Alvirah thought Emmy looked about 16.

'That man who just left,' Emmy stammered. 'Who was he?'

'Carleton Rumson, the producer,' Alvirah said quickly. 'Why?'

'Because . . .' Emmy pulled off her glasses, revealing swollen eyes.

Alvirah put firm hands on the girl's shoulders. 'Emmy, what is it?'

'I don't know what to do,' Emmy wailed. 'I don't know what to do.'

Carleton Rumson returned to his apartment. Beads of perspiration stood on his forehead. That Alvirah Meehan was no dope. That crack about champagne hadn't been social chitchat. How much did she suspect?

Victoria was standing on the terrace, her hands lightly touching the railing. Reluctantly he joined her. 'For Pete's sake, haven't you read those signs all over the place?' he demanded. 'One good shove and that railing would be gone.'

Victoria was wearing white slacks and a white knit sweater. Sourly Rumson thought it was a damn shame some fashion columnist had once written that with her pale-blonde beauty, Victoria Rumson should never wear anything except white. Victoria had taken that advice to heart.

She turned to him calmly. 'I've always noticed that you get ugly with me when you're upset. Did you know Fiona Winters was staying in this building? Perhaps it was at your request.'

'Vic, I haven't seen Fiona in nearly two years. If you don't believe me, too bad.'

'As long as you didn't see her yesterday, darling. I understand the police are asking a lot of questions. It's bound to come out that you and she were, as the columnists say, an item. Have you followed up on Brian McCormack's play? I have one of my famous hunches about that.'

Rumson cleared his throat. 'That Alvirah Meehan is going to have McCormack send me the play. After I've read it I'll go down and meet him.'

'Let me read it too. Then I might just tag along. I'd love to see how a cleaning woman decorates.' Victoria Rumson linked her arm in her husband's. 'Poor darling. Why are you so nervous?'

When Brian rushed into the apartment, his play under his arm, Emmy was lying on the couch, covered by a light blanket. Alvirah closed the door behind him and watched as he knelt beside Emmy and put his arms around her. 'I'm going inside and let you two talk,' she announced.

Willy was in the bedroom laying out clothes. 'Which jacket, honey?' He held up two sports coats.

Alvirah's forehead puckered. 'You want to look nice for Pete's retirement party, but not like you're trying to show off. Wear the blue jacket and the white sports shirt.'

'I still don't like to leave you tonight,' Willy protested.

'You can't miss Pete's dinner,' Alvirah said firmly. 'And Willy, if you have too good a time, I want you to promise me not to drive home. Stay at the old apartment. You know how you can get when you're with the boys.'

Willy smiled sheepishly. 'You mean if I sing "Danny Boy" more than twice, that's my signal.'

'Exactly,' Alvirah said firmly.

'Honey, I'm so bushed after the trip and with what happened last night, I'd just as soon have a few beers with Pete and then come back.'

'That wouldn't be nice. Pete stayed at our lottery-winning party till the morning rush started on the expressway. Now we've got to talk to those kids.'

In the living room Brian and Emmy were sitting side by side, their hands clasped. 'Have you two straightened things out yet?' Alvirah demanded.

'Not exactly,' Brian said. 'Apparently Emmy was given a rough time by Detective Rooney when she refused to answer his questions.'

Alvirah switched on her microphone. 'I have to know everything he asked you.'

Hesitantly Emmy told her. Her voice became calmer and her poise returned as she said, 'Brian, you're going to be indicted. He's trying to make me say things that will hurt you.'

'You mean you're protecting me.' Brian looked astonished. 'There's no need. I haven't done anything. I thought . . .'

'You thought that Emmy was in trouble,' Alvirah told them. She settled with Willy on the opposite side of the couch, facing them. She realized that Brian and Emmy were sitting directly in front of the place on the cocktail table where the fingerprints had been smeared. The drapery was slightly to the right. To someone sitting on this couch, the tieback would have been in full view. 'I'm going to tell you two something,' she announced. 'You each think the other might have had something to do with this – and you're both wrong. Just tell me what you know or think you know. Brian, is there anything you've held back about seeing Fiona Winters yesterday?'

'Absolutely nothing,' Brian said.

'All right. Emmy, your turn.'

Emmy walked over to the window. 'I love this view.' She turned to Alvirah and Willy. 'I've been here a few times. Yesterday when Fiona left my apartment to

157

meet Brian I think I went a little crazy. He had been so involved with her. Fiona is – was the kind of woman who can just beckon to men. I was so afraid Brian would take up with her again.'

'I'd never . . . ' Brian protested.

'Keep quiet, Brian,' Alvirah ordered.

'I sat on the park bench a long time,' Emmy said. 'I saw Brian leave. When Fiona didn't come down I started to think maybe Brian had told her to wait. Finally I decided to have it out with her. I came up in the service elevator because I didn't want anyone to know I'd been here. I rang the doorbell and waited and rang it again and then I left.'

'That's all?' Brian asked. 'Why were you afraid to tell that to Detective Rooney?'

'Because when she heard Fiona was dead she thought maybe the reason she didn't answer was because you'd already killed her.' Alvirah leaned forward. 'Emmy, why did you ask about Carleton Rumson before? You saw him yesterday, didn't you?'

'As I came down the corridor he was ahead of me going toward the passenger elevator. I knew he looked familiar but didn't recognize him until I saw him again just now.'

Alvirah stood up. 'I think we should call Mr. Rumson and ask him to come down, and I think we should call Detective Rooney and ask him to be here too. But first, Brian, give Willy your play. He'll run it up to the Rumson's apartment. Let's see. It's nearly five P.M. Willy, ask Mr. Rumson to phone when he's ready to bring it back.'

The intercom buzzer sounded. Willy answered it. 'Detective Rooney's here,' he said. 'He's looking for you, Brian.'

There was no trace of warmth in Rooney's manner. 'Mr. McCormack, I'm going to ask you to come down

158

to the station house for further questioning. You have received the Miranda warning. I would again remind you that anything you say can be used against you.'

'He's not going anywhere,' Alvirah said firmly. 'Detective Rooney, I've got an earful for you.'

It was nearly seven P.M., two hours later, when Carleton Rumson phoned. Alvirah and Willy had told Detective Rooney about the champagne and the glasses and the fingerprints on the cocktail table and about Emmy seeing Carleton Rumson, but Alvirah could tell none of it cut much ice with Rooney. He's closing his mind to everything that doesn't fit his theory about Brian, she thought.

A few minutes later, Alvirah was astonished to see both Rumsons enter her apartment. Victoria Rumson was smiling warmly. When introduced to Brian, she took both his hands and said, 'You are a young Neil Simon. I read your play. Congratulations.'

When Detective Rooney was introduced, Carleton Rumson's face went ashen. He stammered as he said to Brian, 'I'm terribly sorry to interrupt you just now. I'll make this very brief. Your play is wonderful. I want to option it. Please have your agent contact my office tomorrow.'

Victoria Rumson was standing at the terrace door. 'You were so wise not to cover this view,' she told Alvirah. 'My decorator put in curtains and blinds and I might as well be facing an alley.'

She sure took her gracious pills this morning, Alvirah thought.

'I think we'd all better sit down,' Detective Rooney suggested.

'Mr. Rumson, you knew Fiona Winters,' Detective Rooney said.

Alvirah began to think she had underestimated Rooney. His expression became intense as he leaned forward.

'Miss Winters appeared in several of my productions some years ago,' Rumson said.

He was sitting on one of the couches next to his wife. Alvirah noticed that he glanced at her nervously.

'I'm not interested in years ago,' Rooney told him. 'I'm interested in yesterday. Did you see her?'

'I did not.' To Alvirah, Rumson sounded strained and defensive.

'Did she phone you from this apartment?' Alvirah asked.

'Mrs. Meehan, if you don't mind, I'll conduct this questioning,' the detective said.

'Show respect when you talk to my wife,' Willy bristled.

'I just meant that if she did phone from here, there'll be a record of it so I hate to see Mr. Rumson get in trouble by lying,' Alvirah injected.

Victoria Rumson patted her husband's arm.

'Darling, I think you may be trying to spare my feelings. If that impossible Winters woman was badgering you again, please don't be afraid to tell exactly what she wanted.'

Before their eyes, Rumson seemed to age visibly. When he spoke his voice was weary. 'As I just told you, Fiona Winters acted in several of my productions. She . . .'

'She also had a private relationship with you,' Alvirah interjected. 'You used to take her to the Cypress Point Spa.'

'I haven't had anything to do with Fiona Winters for several years,' Rumson said. 'Yes, she phoned yesterday just about noon. She told me she had a play she wanted me to read. Assured me it had the earmarks of a hit and she wanted to play the lead. I was expecting a call from Europe and agreed to come down and see her in about an hour.'

'That means she called after Brian left,' Alvirah said triumphantly. 'That's why the glasses and champagne were out. They were for you.'

'Did you come to this apartment, Mr. Rumson?' Rooney asked.

Again Rumson hesitated.

'Darling, it's all right,' Victoria Rumson said softly.

Not daring to look at Detective Rooney, Alvirah announced: 'Emmy saw you in this corridor a few minutes after one P.M.'

Rumson sprang to his feet. 'Mrs. Meehan, I won't tolerate any more insinuations! I was afraid Fiona would keep contacting me if I didn't set her straight. I came down here and rang the bell. There was no answer. The door wasn't completely shut, so I pushed it open and called her. As long as I was this far I wanted to be finished with it.'

'Did you enter the apartment?' Rooney asked.

'Yes. I walked through this room, poked my head in the kitchen and glanced in the bedroom. She wasn't anywhere. I hoped she'd changed her mind about seeing me, and I can assure you I was relieved. Then when I heard the news this morning all I could think of was that maybe her body was in that closet when I was here and I'd be in the middle of this.' He turned to his wife. 'I guess I am in the middle of it, but I swear that's true.'

Victoria touched his hand. 'There's no way they're going to drag you into this. What a nerve that woman had to think she should have the leading role in *Nebraska Nights*.' Victoria turned to Emmy. 'Someone your age should play Diane.'

'She's going to,' Brian said. 'I just hadn't told her yet.'

Rooney folded his notebook. 'Mr. Rumson, I'll ask you to accompany me down to headquarters. Miss

161

Laker, I'd like you to give a complete statement as well. Mr. McCormack, we need to talk to you again and I do strongly urge you to engage counsel.'

'Now just one minute,' Alvirah said indignantly. 'I can tell you believe Mr. Rumson over Brian.' There goes the option on the play, but this is more important, she thought. 'You're going to say that Brian maybe started to leave, decided to come back and tell Fiona to clear out and then ended up killing her. I'll tell you how I think it happened. Rumson came down here and got into an argument with Fiona. He strangled her, but was smart enough to take the script she was showing him.'

'That is absolutely untrue,' Rumson snapped.

'I don't want another word discussed here,' Rooney ordered. 'Miss Laker, Mr. Rumson, Mr. McCormack, I have a car downstairs.'

When the door closed behind them Willy put his arms around Alvirah. 'Honey, I'm going to skip Pete's party. I can't leave you. You look ready to collapse.'

Alvirah hugged him back. 'No, you're not. I've been recording everything. I need to listen to the playback and I do that better alone. You have a good time.'

'I know – if I sing "Danny Boy" more than twice, sleep at the old place.'

The apartment felt terribly quiet after Willy left. Alvirah decided that a warm soak in the bathtub Jacuzzi might take some of the stiffness out of her body and clear her brain.

Afterward, she dressed comfortably in her favorite nightgown and Willy's striped terry-cloth robe. She set the expensive cassette player her editor at the *New York Globe* had bought for her on the dining-room table, then took the tiny cassette out of her sunburst pin, inserted it in the recorder and pushed the playback button. She put a new cassette in the back of the pin and fastened the pin to the robe just in case she wanted to think out loud. She sat listening to her conversations with Brian, with Detective Rooney, with Emmy, with the Rumsons.

What was it about Carleton Rumson that bothered her so much? Methodically Alvirah reviewed that first meeting with the Rumsons. He was pretty cool that night, but when we bumped into him the next morning he sure had changed his tune, even reminded me he wanted to read the new play right away. She remembered Brian saying that nobody could get to Carleton Rumson.

That's it, she thought. He already knew how good the play was. He couldn't admit that he'd already read it. Wait until I convince Detective Rooney of this.

The phone rang. Startled, Alvirah hurried over to pick it up. It was Emmy. 'Mrs. Meehan,' she whispered, 'they're still questioning Brian and Mr. Rumson, but I know they think Brian's guilty.'

'I just figured everything out,' Alvirah said triumphantly. 'How good a look at Carleton Rumson did you get when you saw him in the hall?'

'Pretty good.'

'Then you could see he was carrying the script, couldn't you? I mean if he was telling the truth that he only went down to tell Fiona off he'd never have picked up that script. But if they talked about it and he read some of it before he killed her, he'd have taken it. Emmy, I think I've solved the case.'

Emmy's voice was barely audible. 'Mrs. Meehan, I swear Carleton Rumson wasn't carrying anything when I saw him. Suppose Detective Rooney thinks to ask me that question? It's going to hurt Brian when I tell him the truth.'

'You have to tell the truth,' Alvirah said sadly. 'Don't worry. I still have my thinking cap on.' When she hung up, she turned the cassette player on again and began to replay her tapes. She replayed her conversations with Brian several times. There was something he had told her that she was missing.

Finally she stood up, deciding that a breath of fresh air wouldn't hurt. Not that New York air is fresh, she thought as she opened the terrace door and stepped out. This time she went right to the panel and let her fingers rest on the guardrail. If Willy were here he'd have a fit, she thought, but I'm not going to lean on it. There's just something so restful about looking out over the park. I think one of the happiest memories in Mama's life was the day she had a sleigh ride through the park when she was sixteen. She always talked about it. It was because her girlfriend, Beth, asked for that for her birthday.

Beth!

Beth!

That's it, Alvirah thought. Again she could hear Brian saying that Fiona Winters wanted to play the part of Diane. Then Brian corrected himself and said, I mean Beth. Willy asked who's that and Brian said the name of the lead in his new play, that he'd changed it in the final draft. Alvirah switched on her microphone and cleared her throat. Better get this all down. It would help to have her immediate impression when she wrote the story up for the *Globe*. 'It wasn't Rumson who killed Fiona Winters,' she said, her voice confident. 'It was his wife, see-no-evil-Vicky. She was the one who kept after Rumson to read the play. She was the one who said Emmy should play Diane. She didn't know Brian had changed the name. She must have listened in when Fiona phoned him. She came while he waited for his calls from Europe. She didn't want Fiona to get involved with Rumson again so she killed her, then took the script. That was the copy she read, not the final draft.'

'How very clever of you, Mrs. Meehan.'

The voice came from directly behind her. Alvirah felt strong hands at the small of her back. She tried to turn and felt her body press against the guardrailing and panel. How did Victoria Rumson get in here, she wondered, then in a flash remembered that Brian's key had been on the table. With all her strength she tried to throw herself against her attacker, but a blow on the side of her neck stunned her. She spun around and sagged against the railing. Only vaguely was she aware of a creaking, tearing sound and Willy's voice frantically calling her.

Willy hadn't stayed to sing even one chorus of 'Danny Boy'. After dinner, a few beers and a chance to congratulate Pete, something was bugging him that told him to go home. He froze when he entered the apartment and saw the struggling figures at the terrace railing. Shouting Alvirah's name, he rushed across the room.

'Come in, honey,' he pleaded, 'get back.'

Then he realized what the other woman was doing. He took one step out onto the terrace, saw a section of the wall separate and fall, leaving a yawning space next to Alvirah. Willy took a second step toward it and passed out.

Beth! Diane! All the way from the police station to Central Park South, Emmy sat on the edge of the cab seat. She'd been in the precinct waiting for her statement to be typed up, heartsick with worry about Brian, remembering the way he'd looked at her when he told Victoria Rumson that she was going to have the lead in his new play. I don't care about playing Diane as long as Brian's all right, she'd thought. Not Diane. Brian changed the name to Beth. Then in her mind she heard Victoria Rumson say, 'You should play the part of Diane.' That was when it all fit. Victoria Rumson, wildly jealous of her husband, Victoria who had almost lost him to Fiona a couple of years ago.

Emmy had jumped up and run from the station house. She had to talk to Alvirah before she said anything to the cops. She heard a policeman call after her but didn't answer him as she hailed the cab.

When she reached the building, she raced to the elevator. She heard Willy shouting as she came down the corridor. The door was open. She saw Willy go out on the terrace and fall. She saw the silhouettes of two women and realized what was happening.

In a burst of speed Emmy rushed out to the terrace. Alvirah was facing her, swaying over the open space. Her right hand was grasping the part of the railing that was still in place. Victoria Rumson was pummeling that hand with her fists.

Emmy grabbed Victoria's arms and twisted them behind her. Victoria's howl of rage and pain rose above the crash of the terrace wall as it fell to the street. Emmy shoved her aside and managed to grasp the cord of Alvirah's robe. Alvirah was teetering. Her bedroom slippers were sliding backward off the terrace. Her body swayed as she hovered 34 stories over the sidewalk below. With a burst of strength, Emmy pulled her forward and they fell together over the collapsed form of the unconscious Willy.

Alvirah and Willy slept until noon. When they finally awakened, Willy insisted Alvirah stay put. He went out to the kitchen, returning fifteen minutes later with a pitcher of orange juice, a pot of tea and a plate of toast. After her second cup of tea, Alvirah regained her customary optimism. 'Boy, was it good that Detective Rooney came barging in here after Emmy and caught

Victoria Rumson trying to escape. And do you know what I think, Willy?'

'I never know what to think, honey,' Willy sighed.

'One of the reasons Carleton Rumson never wanted a divorce is because he didn't want to split his money. With see-no-evil-Vicky in jail he won't have to worry about that. And I bet anything that he still produces Brian's play.

'And Willy,' Alvirah concluded, 'I want you to have a talk with Brian to tell him he'd better marry that darling Emmy before somebody else snaps her up.' She beamed. 'I have the perfect wedding present for them, a load of white furniture.'

The doorbell rang. Willy struggled into his robe and hurried out. When he opened the door, Brian and Emmy came in. Willy took one look at their radiant faces and entwined hands and said, 'I hope your favorite color is white.'

Plumbing for Willy

If Alvirah Meehan had been able to look into a crystal ball and watch the events of the next ten days unfold, she would have grabbed Willy by the hand and raced out of the green room. Instead she sat and chatted with the other guests of the Phil Donahue program. Today the subject was not sex orgies or battered husbands but people who had messed up their lives by winning big in the lottery.

The support group for lottery winners had been contacted by the Donahue show and now the worst-case guests had been chosen. Alvirah and Willy would be a counterpoint to the others, the interviewer told them. 'Whatever she means by that,' Alvirah commented to Willy after their initial interview.

For her appearance, Alvirah had her hair freshly colored to the soft strawberry shade that softened her angular face. This morning Willy had told her that she looked exactly the same as she did when he'd first laid eyes on her at a Knights of Columbus dance more than forty years ago. Baroness Min von Schreiber had flown into New York from the Cypress Point Spa in Pebble Beach to select Alvirah's outfit for the broadcast. 'Be sure to mention that the first thing you did when you won the lottery was to come to the Spa,' she cautioned Alvirah. 'With this damn recession business is not so brisk.'

Alvirah was wearing a pale blue silk suit with a white

blouse and her signature sunburst pin. She wished she'd managed to lose the twenty pounds she'd regained when she and Willy went to Spain in August, but still Alvirah knew she looked very nice. Very nice for her, that was. She had no illusions that with her slightly jutting jaw and broad frame she'd ever be tapped to compete in the Mrs. America contest.

There were two other sets of guests; three co-workers in a pantyhose factory who'd shared a ten million dollar ticket six years ago. They'd decided their luck was so good that they should buy race-horses with their winnings and were now broke. Their future checks were owed to the banks and Uncle Sam. The other winners, a couple, had won sixteen million dollars, bought a hotel in Vermont, and were now slaving seven days a week trying to keep up with the overhead. Any leftover money was used to place classified ads trying to dump the hotel on someone else.

An assistant came to bring them into the studio.

Alvirah was used to being on television now. She knew enough to sit at a slight angle so she looked a little thinner. She didn't wear chunky jewelry that could rustle against the microphone. She kept her sentences short.

Willy, on the other hand, could never get used to being in the public eye. Even though Alvirah always assured him he was a grand-looking man and people did take him for Tip O'Neill, he was happiest with a ratchet in his hand fixing a leaking pipe. Willy was a born plumber.

Donahue began in his usual breezy, slightly incredulous voice. 'Can you believe that after you win millions of dollars in the lottery you need a support group? Can you believe that you can be broke even though you have big fat checks still coming in?'

'Nah,' the studio audience dutifully shrieked.

Alvirah remembered to tuck her stomach in then reached for Willy's hand and entwined his fingers in hers. She didn't want him to look nervous on the television screen. A lot of their family and friends would be watching. Sister Cordelia, Willy's oldest sister, had invited a whole crowd of retired nuns to the convent to see the show.

Three men observing the program with avid interest were not Donahue's usual viewers. Sammy, Clarence and Tony had just been released from the maximum security prison near Albany where they'd been guests of the state for twelve years for their part in the armed robbery of a Brink's truck. Unfortunately for them they never got to spend their six hundred thousand dollar heist. The getaway car had blown a tire a block from the scene of the crime.

Now, having paid their debt to society, they were looking for a new way to get rich. The idea of kidnapping the relative of a lottery winner was Clarence's brainchild. That was why they were watching Donahue today from their seedy room in the shabby Lincoln Arms Hotel on Ninth Avenue and Fortieth Street. Tony at thirty-five was ten years younger than the others. Like his brother, Sammy, he was barrelchested, with powerful arms. Small eyes disappeared into the folds of flesh from hooded lids. His thick dark hair was unkempt. He obeyed his brother blindly and his brother obeyed Clarence.

Clarence was a total contrast to the others. Small, wiry, and soft-voiced he emitted a chilling aura. With good reason people were instinctively afraid of him. Clarence had been born without a conscience, and a number of unsolved homicides would have been cleared from the books if he had talked in his sleep during his incarceration.

Sammy had never admitted to Clarence that Tony

170

had been joyriding in the getaway car the night before the Brink's robbery and had run through a street full of glass. Tony would not have lived to express his regret that he hadn't checked the tires.

One of the lottery winners who'd invested in the horses was whining, 'There wasn't enough money in the world to feed those nags.' His partners nodded vigorously.

Sammy snorted, 'Those jerks can't rub two nickels together.' He reached to turn off the set.

'Wait a minute,' Clarence snapped.

Alvirah was speaking. 'We weren't used to money,' she explained. 'I mean, we lived a nice life. We had a three-room apartment in Flushing and still keep it just in case the state goes broke and tells us to take a flying leap for the rest of our checks. But I was a cleaning woman and Willy a plumber and we had to be careful.'

'Plumbers make a fortune,' Donahue protested.

'Not Willy,' Alvirah smiled. 'He spent at least half his time fixing things free at rectories and convents and for people who were hard up. You know how it is. It's so expensive to get sinks and toilets and tubs working and Willy felt that this was his way of making life easier for other people. He still does it.'

'Well, surely you've had some fun with the money?' Donahue asked. 'You're very well dressed.'

Alvirah remembered to get in a plug for the Cypress Point Spa as she explained that, yes indeed, they had fun. They'd bought an apartment on Central Park South. They traveled a lot. They gave to charity. She wrote articles for the *New York Globe* and she'd been fortunate enough to solve some crimes along the way. She'd always wanted to be a detective. 'Nevertheless,' she concluded firmly, 'in the five years since we've been winners we've saved half of every single check. And that money is all in the bank.'

Clarence, followed by Sammy and Tony, joined in the vigorous applause of the studio audience. Clarence was smiling now, a thin, mirthless smile. 'Two million bucks a year. Let's say almost half of that for taxes so that means they net a little over a million bucks a year and save half of that. They gotta have two million plus in the bank. That oughta keep us going for a while.'

'We snatch her?' Tony asked pointing at the screen.

Clarence withered him with a glance. 'No, you dope. Look at the two of them. He's hanging on to her like she's a life preserver. He'd fall apart and go running to the cops. We take him. She'll take orders and pay to get him back.' He looked around. 'I hope Willy enjoys staying with us.'

Tony frowned. 'We gotta keep him blindfolded. I don't want him picking me out of no line-up.'

It was Sammy who sighed. 'Tony, don't worry about it. The minute we get the money, Willy Meehan will be looking for leaks in the Hudson River.'

Two weeks later, Alvirah was having her hair done at Louis Vincent, the salon around the corner from the Central Park South apartment. 'Since the program was aired, I'm getting so many letters,' she told Vincent. 'Do you know I even got one from the President? He congratulated us on our wise handling of our finances. He said we were a perfect example of trickle-up prosperity. I wish he'd invited us to a White House dinner. I've always wanted to go to one of those. Well, maybe someday.'

'Just make sure I do your hair,' Vincent admonished as he gave a final touch to Alvirah's coiffure. 'Are you having a manicure?'

Afterward Alvirah knew she should have listened to the queer feeling that suggested she get back to the apartment. She would have caught Willy before he rushed into the car with those men.

Half an hour later when the doorman saw her, he broke into a relieved smile. 'Mrs. Meehan, it must have been a mistake. Your husband looked so worried.'

Incredulous, Alvirah listened as Jose told her that Willy had come running from the elevator in tears. He'd yelled that Alvirah had a heart attack under the dryer and had been rushed to Roosevelt Hospital.

'A guy was outside in a black Cadillac,' Jose said. 'He pulled into the driveway when I opened the door. The doctor sent his own car for Mr. Meehan.'

'That sounds funny,' Alvirah said slowly. 'I'll get over to the hospital right away.'

'I'll call a cab,' the doorman told her. His phone rang. With an apologetic smile, he picked it up. 'Two-eleven Central Park South.' He listened, then, looking puzzled, said, 'It's for you, Mrs. Meehan.'

'Me?' Alvirah grabbed the phone and with a sinking heart heard a whispered voice say, 'Alvirah, listen carefully. Tell the doorman your husband is fine. It was all a misunderstanding. He's going to meet you later. Then go upstairs to your apartment and wait for instructions.'

Willy had been kidnapped. Alvirah knew it. Oh God, she thought. 'That's fine,' she managed to say. 'Tell Willy I'll meet him in an hour.'

'You're a very smart woman, Mrs. Meehan,' the voice whispered.

There was a click in her ear. Alvirah turned to Jose.

'Complete mistake of course. Poor Willy.' She tried to laugh. 'Ah . . . ha . . . ha . . .'

Jose beamed. 'In Puerto Rico I never once hear about a doctor sending his car.'

The apartment was on the twenty-second floor and

173

had a terrace overlooking Central Park. Usually Alvirah smiled the minute she opened the door. The apartment was so pretty, and if she said so herself, she had an eye for furniture. All those years of cleaning other people's houses had been an education in interior design.

But today she took no comfort in the matching ivory couch and loveseat, Willy's deep comfortable chair with its own ottoman, the crimson red and royal blue oriental carpet, the black lacquered table and chairs in the dining area, the late afternoon sun that danced across the blanket of autumn leaves in the park.

What good was any of it if anything happened to Willy? With all her heart, Alvirah fiercely wished they'd never won the lottery and were back in their Flushing apartment over Orazio Romano's tailor shop. It was at this time she'd be coming home from cleaning Mrs. O'Keefe's house and joking to Willy that Mrs. O'Keefe had been vaccinated with a Victrola needle. 'Willy, she never shuts up. Even shouts over the vacuum. It's a good thing she isn't messy. I'd never get the work done.'

The phone rang. Alvirah rushed to pick up the extension in the living room then changed her mind and in stumbling haste ran into the bedroom. The recording machine was there. She pushed the record button as she picked up the phone.

It was the same whispery voice. 'Alvirah?'

'Yes. Where's Willy? Whatever you do, don't hurt him.' She could hear background sounds like planes taking off. Was Willy at an airport?

'We won't hurt him as long as we get the money and as long as you don't call the cops. You didn't call them, did you?'

'No. I want to talk to Willy.'

174

'In a minute. How much money have you got in the bank?'

'Something over two million dollars.'

'You're an honest woman, Alvirah. That's just about what we figured. If you want Willy back you'd better start making some withdrawals.'

'You can have it all.'

There was a low chuckle. 'I like you, Alvirah. Two million is fine. Take it out in cash. Don't give a hint that anything is wrong. No marked money, baby. And don't go to the cops. We'll be watching you.'

The airport sounds became almost deafening. 'I can't hear you,' Alvirah said desperately. 'And I'm not giving you one cent until I'm sure that Willy is still alive.'

'Talk to him.'

A minute later a sheepish voice said, 'Hi, honey.'

Relief, total and overwhelming, flooded Alvirah. Her ever-resourceful brain, which had been inactive since Jose told her about Willy getting in the 'doctor's car', resumed its normal steel-trap efficiency.

'Honey,' she yelled so that his abductors could hear, 'tell those guys to take good care of you. Otherwise they won't get a plug nickel.'

Willy's hands were tied together. So were his feet. He watched as the boss, Clarence, put his thumb on the handset and the connection broke. 'That's quite a woman you have, Willy,' Clarence said. Then Clarence turned off the machine that simulated airport background.

Willy felt like a jerk. If Alvirah had really had a heart attack, Louis or Vincent would have called him from the salon. He should have known that. What a dope he was. He looked around. This was some crummy dump. When he got in the car the guy who was hiding in the backseat put a gun in his neck. 'Try to make trouble and I blow you away.' The gun was jostling against him when they hustled him through the lobby, up the rickety elevator of this crummy joint. It was only a block from the Lincoln Tunnel. The windows were closed tight, but even so the exhaust fumes from the buses and trucks and cars were overwhelming. You could practically see them.

Willy had sized up Tony and Sammy fast. Not too much upstairs. He might be able to give them the slip somehow. But when Clarence came in, announcing that he'd warned Alvirah to let the doorman think everything was hunky-dory, Willy felt his first real fear. Clarence reminded him of Nutsy, a guy he'd known as a kid. Nutsy used to shoot his BB gun into birds' nests.

It was obvious Clarence was the boss. He called Alvirah and talked to her about the ransom. He made the decision to put Willy on the phone. Now he said, 'Put him back in the closet.'

'Hey, wait a minute,' Willy protested. 'I'm starving.'

'We're gonna order hamburgers and french fries,' Sammy told him as he slipped a gag over Willy's mouth. 'We'll letcha eat.'

Sammy trussed Willy's feet and legs in a spiral sequence of cord and knots and shoved him in the narrow closet. The door did not seal against the frame and Willy could hear the low-toned conversation. 'Two million bucks means she has to go to twenty banks. She's too smart to leave more than a hundred thou' in any of them. That's how much is insured. Figuring the forms she has to fill out and the bank, counting the money, give her three, four days to get it.'

'She'll need four,' Clarence said. 'We get the money by Friday night. We tell her we're gonna count it and then she can pick up Willy.' He laughed. 'Then we send her a map with X mark to show where to start dredging.'

Alvirah sat for hours in Willy's chair, staring unseeingly as the late afternoon sun sent slanting shadows over Central Park. The last lingering rays disappeared. She reached to turn on the lamp and got up slowly. It was no use thinking of all the good times she and Willy had had these forty years or that just this morning they were going through brochures to decide on whether to take a camel trip through India or a balloon safari in western Africa.

I'm going to get him back, she decided, her jaw jutting out a little more aggressively. The first thing she had to do was to make a cup of tea. The next was to get out all the bankbooks and lay a plan for going from one bank to another and withdrawing cash.

The banks were scattered all over Manhattan and Queens. One hundred thousand dollar deposits in each of them and, of course, accumulated interest, which they took out at the end of the year and used to start a new account. 'No, double the money schemes for us,' they'd agreed. In the bank. Insured. Period. When someone had tried to talk them into buying zero bonds that paid off in ten or fifteen years, Alvirah had said, 'At our age we don't buy things that pay off in ten years.'

She smiled, remembering that Willy had chimed in, 'And we don't buy green bananas either.'

Alvirah swallowed a giant lump in her throat as she sipped the tea and decided that tomorrow morning she'd start on Fifty-seventh Street at Chase Manhattan, go across the street to Chemical, work her way along Park Avenue starting at Citibank and then hit Wall Street.

177

It was a long night lying awake wondering if Willy was okay. I'm going to make them let me talk to him every night until I get all the money, she promised herself. That way they won't hurt him till I figure something out.

At dawn she was becoming tempted to call the police. By the time she got up, at seven, she'd decided against it. These people might have a spy in the building who would report if there was a lot of activity in the apartment. She couldn't take a chance.

Willy spent the night in the closet. They loosened the ropes enough for him to stretch out a little. But they didn't give him a blanket or pillow and his head was resting on someone's shoe. There was no way to push it aside. There was too much junk in the closet. When he dozed off occasionally he dreamt that his neck was embedded on the side of Mount Rushmore directly below the sculpture of Teddy Roosevelt's face.

The banks didn't open till nine. By eight-thirty, Alvirah, in a burst of pressure-cooker energy, had cleaned the already clean apartment. Her bankbooks were in her voluminous shoulder bag. She had dug from the closet a frankfurter-shaped plastic carry-all, the one remnant on Central Park South of the days when she and Willy spent their vacations taking Greyhounds tours to the Catskills.

The October morning was crisp and Alvirah was wearing a light green suit that she'd bought when she was on one of her diets. The waistband wouldn't close, but a large pin solved that problem. Automatically she fastened her sunburst pin with the concealed recorder on the lapel.

It was still too early to leave. Trying to keep up the positive thinking that everything would be hunky-dory as soon as the money was paid, Alvirah reheated the kettle and turned on the CBS morning news.

For once the headlines were fairly mundane. There was no bigshot Mafia guy on trial. No fatal attraction homicide. Nobody had been arrested for selling phony junk bonds.

Alvirah sipped her tea and was about to hit the 'Off' button when the newscaster announced that as of today, New Yorkers could use the device that recorded the phone number of incoming callers within the 212 area code.

It took a minute for her to realize what that meant. Then Alvirah jumped up and ran to the utility closet. Among the other electronic devices that she and Willy delighted in taking home from Hammacher Schlemmer was the recording machine that listed incoming phone numbers. They'd bought it not realizing it was useless in New York.

Dear Lord and his Blessed Mother, she prayed as she ripped the box open, pulled out the recorder and with trembling fingers substituted it for the answering machine in the bedroom. Let them be keeping Willy in New York. Let them call from wherever they're hiding him.

She remembered to record an announcement. 'You have reached the home of Alvirah and Willy Meehan. At the beep please leave a message. We'll get back to you real soon.' She played it back. Her voice sounded different, worried, full of stress.

She forced herself to remember that she had won the dramatic medal in the sixth-grade play at St Francis Xavier School in the Bronx. Be an actress, she told herself firmly. She took a deep breath and began again: 'Hell-lo. You have reached the home . . .'

That's more like it, she decided when she listened to the new version. Then, clutching her shoulder bag,

179

Alvirah headed for Chase Manhattan Bank to begin to put together Willy's ransom money.

I'm gonna go nuts, Willy thought as he tried to flex arms that somehow managed to be both numb and aching. His legs were still firmly trussed together. He'd given up on them. At eight-thirty he heard a faint rapping. Probably what passed for room service in this dump. They brought up lousy food on paper plates. At least that was the way the hamburgers had been delivered last night. Even so, the thought of a cup of coffee and a piece of toast set Willy's mouth to watering.

A moment later the closet door opened. Sammy and Tony were staring down at him. Sammy held the gun while Tony released Willy's gag. 'Didja have a good night's sleep?' Tony's unlovely smile revealed a broken eyetooth.

Willy longed to have his hand free for just two minutes. They itched to give Tony a matching set of eyeteeth. 'Slept like a baby,' he lied. He nodded in the direction of the bathroom. 'How about it?'

'What?' Tony blinked, his rubbery face drooping in puzzlement.

'He needs to go to the head,' Clarence said. He crossed the narrow room and bent over Willy. 'See that gun?' He pointed to it. 'It has a silencer. You try anything funny and it's all over. Sammy has a very nervous trigger finger. Then we'll all be mad because you gave us so much trouble. And we'll have to take it out on your wife. Get it?'

Willy was absolutely certain that Clarence meant it. Tony might be dopey. Sammy might have a trigger finger but he wouldn't do anything without getting the okay from Clarence. And Clarence was a killer. He tried to sound calm. 'I get it.'

180

Somehow he managed to hobble to the bathroom. Tony loosened his hands enough that he could splash some water in his face. Willy looked around in disgust. The tile was broken and looked as though it hadn't been cleaned in years. Flecks of rust-corroded enamel covered the tub and sink. Worst of all was the constant dripping from the water tank, faucets, and shower head. 'Sounds like Niagara Falls in here,' Willy commented to Tony, who was standing at the door.

Tony shoved him over to where Sammy and Clarence were sitting at a rickety card table, which was piled with containers of coffee and objects that resembled abandoned Egg McMuffins. Clarence nodded to the folding chair next to Sammy. 'Sit there.' Then he whirled. 'Shut that damn door,' he ordered Tony. 'That stinking dripping is driving me nuts. Kept me awake half the night.'

A thought came to Willy. He tried to sound casual. 'I guess we'll be here a couple of days. If you pick up a few tools for me I can fix that for you.' He reached for a container. 'I'm the best plumber you ever kidnapped.'

Alvirah learned that it was much easier to put money in a bank than to get it out. When she presented her withdrawal slip at Chase Manhattan, the teller's eyes bulged. Then he asked her to step over to an assistant manager's desk.

Fifteen minutes later Alvirah was still adamantly insisting that, no, she wasn't unhappy with the service. Yes, she was sure she wanted the money in cash. Yes, she understood what a certified check was. Finally she demanded emphatically, 'Is it my money or isn't it?'

'Of course. Of course.' They would have to ask her to fill out some forms – government regulations for cash withdrawals of over ten thousand dollars.

Then they had to count the money. Eyes popped when Alvirah told them she wanted five hunded hundred-dollar bills and one thousand fifty-dollar bills. That took a lot of counting.

It was nearly noon when Alvirah hailed a cab to cover the three blocks to the apartment, dump the money in a dresser drawer and start out again for the Chemical Bank on Eighth Avenue.

By the end of the day she'd managed to get only three hundred thousand of the two million she needed. Then she sat in the apartment staring at the phone. There was a way to move quicker. In the morning she'd call the rest of the banks and tell them to expect her withdrawals. Start counting now, fellows.

At six-thirty the phone rang. Alvirah grabbed it as a phone number appeared on the surface of the recording machine. A familiar number. Alvirah realized the caller was the formidable Sister Cordelia.

Willy had seven sisters. Six of them had gone in the convent. The seventh, now deceased, was the mother of Brian, the playwright Alvirah and Willy loved as a son. Brian was in London now. Alvirah would have turned to him for help if he'd been in New York.

But she wasn't about to tell Cordelia about Willy's abduction. Cordelia would have the White House on the phone demanding that the President dispatch the standing army to rescue her brother.

Cordelia sounded a little peeved. 'Alvirah, Willy was supposed to come over this afternoon. One of the old girls we visit needs to have her toilet fixed. It's not like him to forget. Let me talk to him.'

Alvirah laughed that same he-har-har laugh that sounded even to her ears like the canned stuff you hear on lousy television shows. 'Cordelia, it must have gone out of his mind,' she said. 'Willy is . . . he's . . . '

She had a burst of inspiration. 'Willy's in Washington to testify about the cheapest way to fix plumbing in the tenements the government is restoring. You know how he can do miracles to make things work. The President read that Willy is a genius at that and sent for him.'

'The President!' Cordelia's incredulous tone made Alvirah wish she'd named Senator Moynihan or maybe some congressman. I never lie, she fretted. I don't know how.

'Willy would never go to Washington without you,' Cordelia snorted.

'They sent a car for him.' Well, at least that's true, Alvirah thought.

She heard the hrrump on the other end of the line. Cordelia was nobody's fool. 'Well, when he gets back, tell him to get right over here.'

Two minutes later the phone rang again. This time the number that came up was not familiar. It's *them*, Alvirah thought. She realized her hand was shaking. Forcing herself to think of the sixth-grade dramatic medal, she reached for the receiver.

Her hello was hardy and confident.

'We hope you've been banking, Mrs. Meehan.'

'Yes, I have. Put Willy on.'

'You can talk to him in a minute. We want the money by Friday night.'

'Friday night! It's Tuesday now. That only gives me three days. It takes a long time to get all that together.'

'Do it. Say hello to Willy.'

'Hi, honey.' Willy's voice sounded subdued. Then he said, 'Hey, let me talk.'

Alvirah heard the sound of the receiver dropping. 'Okay, Alvirah,' the whispery voice said. 'We're not going to call you again until Friday night at seven o'clock. We'll let you talk to Willy then and we'll tell you where to meet us. Remember, any funny business and in the future you'll have to pay to have your plumbing fixed. Willy won't be around to take care of it.'

The receiver clicked in her ear. Willy. Willy. Her hand still gripping the phone, Alvirah stared at the number listed on the machine: 555-7000. Should she call it back? But suppose one of them answered. They'd know she was tracing them. Instead she called the *Globe*. As she expected, her editor, Jim, was still at his desk. She explained what she needed.

'Sure, I can get it for you, Alvirah. You sound kind of mysterious. Are you working on a case you can write up for us?'

'I'm not sure yet.'

Ten minutes later he called back. 'Hey, Alvirah, that's some dump you're looking up. It's the Lincoln Arms Hotel on Ninth Avenue, near the Tunnel. It's one step down from the flop house.'

The Lincoln Arms Hotel. Alvirah managed to thank Jim before she slammed down the phone and headed out the door.

Just in case she was being watched she left the apartment house through the garage and hailed a cab. She started to tell the driver to take her to the hotel, then thought better of it. Suppose one of Willy's kid-nappers spotted her? Instead she had him drop her at the bus terminal. That was only a block away from the Lincoln Tunnel.

Her kerchief covering her head, her coat collar turned up, Alvirah walked past the Lincoln Arms Hotel. Dismayed, she realized it was a pretty big place. She glanced up at the windows. Was Willy behind one of them? The building looked as though it had been built before the Civil War, but it was at least ten or twelve stories high. How could she ever find him in this place? Once again she wondered if she should call the cops and then remembered again the time some wife did and the cops were spotted at the ransom drop and the kidnappers sped away. They found the body three weeks later.

Alvirah stood in the shadows at the side of the hotel and prayed to St Jude, the saint of the impossible. And then she spotted it. A sign in the window. HELP. WANTED. Four to twelve P.M. shift. Room service? She had to get that job, but not looking like this.

Ignoring the trucks and cars and buses that were barreling toward the tunnel entrance, Alvirah dashed into the street, grabbed a cab, and snapped the address of the apartment in Flushing. Her brain was working overtime.

The old apartment had been their home for forty years and looked exactly the same as it had the day they'd won the lottery. The dark gray overstuffed velour couch and matching chair, the green and orange rug the lady she cleaned for on Tuesdays had been throwing out, the mahogany veneer bedroom set that had been Willy's mother's bridal furniture.

In the closet were all the clothes she'd worn in those days. Splashy print dresses from Alexander's. Polyester slacks and sweatshirts, sneakers and high-heeled shoes purchased at outlets. In the mirror cabinet of the bathroom she found the henna rinse that made her hair the color of the rising sun on the Japanese flag.

An hour later there was no vestige left of the gentrified lottery winner. Bright red hair wisped around a face now startling with the makeup she used to love before Baroness Min taught her that less is better. Her old lipstick exactly matched her flaming hair. Her eyes were emblazoned in purple shadow. Dungarees too tight across the seat, ankles hidden by thick socks and stuffed into well-worn sneakers, a fleece-lined sweat-shirt with the skyline of Manhattan emblazoned across the back finished the transformation.

Alvirah surveyed the overall result with satisfaction. I look like someone who'd apply for a job in that crummy hotel, she decided. Reluctantly she left her sunburst pin in a drawer. It just didn't look right on the sweatshirt.

When she pulled on her old all-weather coat she remembered to switch her money and keys to the volu-minous black and green totebag that she'd always carried to her cleaning jobs.

Forty minutes later she was in the Lincoln Arms hotel. The grimy lobby consisted of a battered desk in front of a wall of mailboxes and four black naugahyde chairs in advanced stages of disrepair. The stained brown carpet was covered with gaping holes that re-vealed ancient linoleum flooring.

Never mind room service, they ought to look for a cleaning woman, Alvirah thought as she approached the desk.

The clerk, sallow complexioned, bleary-eyed, looked up.

'Whaddaya want?'

'A job. I'm a good waitress.'

Something that was more sneer than smile moved the clerk's lips. 'You don't need to be good, just fast. How old are ya?'

'Fifty,' Alvirah lied.

'You're fifty. I'm twelve. Go home.'

'I need a job.' Alvirah persisted, her heart pounding. She could feel Willy's presence. She'd have taken an oath that he was hidden somewhere in this hotel. 'Give me a chance. I'll work free for three of four days. If I'm not the best worker you ever had by, let's say Saturday, you can fire me.'

The clerk shrugged. 'So whadda I got to lose? Be here tomorrow at four sharp. Whaddaya say your name was?'

'Tessie,' Alvirah said firmly. 'Tessie Magink.'

Wednesday morning Willy could sense the tension tightening between his captors. Clarence flatly refused to allow Sammy to step outside the room. When Sammy complained, Clarence snapped, 'After twelve years in a cell you shouldn't have no trouble staying put.'

There was no sign of a chambermaid beating down the door to clean the room. But Willy decided it probably hadn't been cleaned in a year anyhow. The three cot-like beds were lined up together, heads against the bathroom wall. A narrow dresser covered with peeling sheets of Contact, a black and white television, and a round table with four chairs completed the decor.

On Tuesday night, Willy had persuaded his captors to allow him to sleep on the bathroom floor. It was bigger than the closet and, as he pointed out, stretched out that extra bit would make it possible for him to be able to walk when they exchanged him for the ransom. He did not miss the glances they exchanged at the suggestion. They had no intention of letting him go free to talk about them. That meant he had about forty-eight hours to figure out a way of being rescued from this fleabag.

At three in the morning when he'd heard Sammy and Tony snoring in harmony and Clarence's irritated but regular gasps, Willy had managed to sit up, get to his feet, and hop over to the toilet. The rope that tethered him to the bathtub faucet allowed him just enough room to touch the lid of the water tank. With his manacled hands he lifted it, laid it on the sink, and reached into the grimy, rust-coated water of the tank.

The result was that a few minutes later the dripping had become louder, more frequent and more insistent.

That was why Clarence had awakened to the distressing sound of constantly bubbling water. Willy smiled a grim, inner smile as Clarence barked, 'I'm gonna go nuts. Sounds like a camel peeing.'

When the room service breakfast was being delivered Willy was again securely tied and gagged in the closet this time with Sammy's gun at his temple. From the hall outside the room, Willy could hear the faint croak of the obviously old man who was apparently the sole room service employee. It was useless to even think about attracting his attention.

That afternoon Clarence began stuffing towels around the bathroom door, but nothing could block out the sound of running water. 'I'm getting one of my bad headaches,' he snarled, settling down on the unmade bed. A few minutes later Tony began to whistle. Sammy shut him up immediately. Willy heard him whisper, 'When Clarence gets one of his headaches, watch out.'

Tony was clearly bored. His ferret eyes glazed over as he sat watching television, the sound barely turned on. Willy sat next to him, tied to the chair, the gag loosened enough that he could talk through almost closed lips.

At the table, Sammy played endless games of solitaire. In the late afternoon, Tony got bored with the television and snapped it off. 'You got any kids?' he asked Willy.

Willy knew that if he had any hope of getting out of this dump alive, Tony would be his ticket. Trying to ignore the combination of cramps and numbness in his arms and legs, he told Tony that he and Alvirah had never been blessed with kids, but they thought of his nephew, Brian, as their own child especially since Brian's mother who was Willy's sister had been called to her eternal reward. 'I have six other sisters,' he explained. 'They're all nuns. Cordelia is the oldest. She's sixty-eight going on twenty-one.'

Tony's jaw dropped. 'No foolin'. When I was a kid and kind of on the streets and picking up a few bucks separating women from their pocketbooks, if you know what I mean, I never once hit on a nun even when they were heading for the supermarket meaning they had cash. When I had a good hit I left a coupla bucks in the convent mailbox, sort of an expression of gratitude.'

Willy tried to look impressed at Tony's largess.

'Will you shut up?' Clarence barked from the bed. 'My head's splitting.'

Willy breathed a silent prayer as he said, 'You know I could fix that leak if I just had a monkey wrench and a screwdriver.'

If he could just get his hands on that tank, he thought. He could flood the joint. They couldn't very well shoot him if people were rushing in to stop the cascade of water he could unloose.

Sister Cordelia knew something was wrong. Much as she loved Willy she could not imagine the President sending for him in a private car. Something else; Alvirah was always so open you could read her like the headline of the *New York Post*. But when Cordelia tried to phone Alvirah Wednesday morning there was no answer. Then, when she did reach her at three-thirty, Alvirah sounded out of breath. She was just running out, she explained, but didn't say where. Of course, Willy was fine. Why wouldn't he be? He'd be home by the weekend.

The convent was an apartment in an old building

on Amsterdam Avenue and 110th Street. Sister Cordelia lived there with four elderly sisters and the one novice, twenty-seven-year-old Sister Maeve Marie who had been a policewoman for three years before realizing she had a vocation.

When Cordelia hung up after speaking to Alvirah she sat down heavily on a sturdy kitchen chair. 'Maeve,' she said, 'something is wrong with Willy. I feel it in my bones.'

The phone rang again. It was Arturo Morales, the manager of the bank in Flushing around the corner from Willy and Alvirah's old apartment.

'Sister,' he began, sounding distressed, 'I hate to bother you, but I'm worried.'

Cordelia's heart sank as Arturo explained that Alvirah had tried to withdraw one hundred thousand dollars from the bank. They were able to give her only twenty but had promised to have the rest Friday morning, when she absolutely needed it by then.

Cordelia thanked him for the information, promised never to hint that he'd violated bank confidentiality, hung up and snapped to Maeve Marie, 'Come on. We're going to see Alvirah.'

Alvirah reported to the Lincoln Arms Hotel promptly at four o'clock. She'd changed her clothes in the Port Authority. Now standing in front of the desk clerk she felt secure in her disguise. The clerk jerked his head to indicate that she was to go down the corridor to the door marked STAY OUT.

It led to the kitchen. The chef, a bony seventy-year-old who bore a startling resemblance to the cowboy star of the 'Forties, Gabby Hayes, was preparing hamburgers. Clouds of smoke rose from the spatters of grease on the grill. He looked up. 'You Tessie?'

Alvirah nodded.

'Okay. I'm Hank. Start delivering.'

There were no subtleties in the room service department. The kind of brown plastic tray that was found in hospital cafeterias, coarse napkins, plastic utensils, sample-sized mustard, ketchup, and relish.

Hank shoveled limp hamburgers on to buns. 'Pour the coffee. Don't fill the cups too much. Dish out the french fries.'

Alvirah obeyed. 'How many rooms in this place?' she asked as she set up trays.

'Hundred.'

'That many!'

Hank grinned, revealing tobacco-stained false teeth. 'Only forty rented overnight. The by-the-hour trade ain't looking for room service.'

Alvirah considered. Forty wasn't too bad. She figured there had to be at least two men involved in the kidnapping. One to drive the car, one to keep Willy from bopping him. Maybe even one more to make that first phone call. She needed to watch for big orders. At least it was a start.

She began delivering with Hank's firm reminder to collect on the spot. The hamburgers went to the bar, which was inhabited by a dozen or so rough-looking guys you wouldn't want to meet on a dark night. The second order she brought to the room clerk and hotel manager, who presided over the premises from an airless room behind the desk. Their heros were on the house. Her next tray, containing cornflakes and a double boilermaker was for a disheveled, bleary-eyed senior citizen. Alvirah was sure the cornflakes were an afterthought.

Next she was sent with a heavy tray to four men playing cards on the ninth floor. Another card game group on the seventh floor ordered pizzas. On the eighth floor she was met at the door by a husky guy

191

who said, 'Oh. You're new. I'll take it. When you knock on the door, don't bang. My brother got a bad headache.' Behind him Alvirah could see a man lying on a bed, a cloth over his eyes. The persistent dripping sound from the bathroom reminded her overwhelmingly of Willy. He'd have that leak fixed in no time flat.

There was clearly no one else in the room and the guy at the door looked as though he could have cleaned the contents of the tray on his own. In the closet Willy could just about hear the cadence of a voice that made him ache to be back with Alvirah.

There were enough room service calls to keep her busy from six until about ten. From her own observations and from the explanations of Hank, who grew increasingly garrulous as he began to appreciate her efficiency, Alvirah got to understand the setup. There were ten floors of rooms, ten rooms to a floor. The first six floors were reserved for the hourly guests. The upper floor rooms were the largest, all with baths, and tended to be rented for at least a few days.

Over a plump hamburger that she cooked for him at ten o'clock, Hank told her that everybody registered under a false name. Everybody paid cash. 'Like one guy who comes in to clean out his private mailboxes. He publishes dirty magazines. 'Nother guy sets up card games. Lots of fellows come in here and get a bag on when they're supposed to be on a business trip. That kind of stuff. Nothing bad. It's sort of like a private club.'

Hank's head was beginning to droop after he'd finished the last of his third glass of beer. A few minutes later he was asleep. Quietly Alvirah went to the table that served as a combination chopping board and desk. When she brought down the money after each order was delivered she'd been instructed to put it in the cigar box that served as cash register. The order slip with the amount was placed in the box next to it. Hank had explained that at midnight, room service ended and the desk clerk tallied up the money, compared it with the receipts, and put the cash in the safe, which was hidden in the bottom of the refrigerator. The order slips were then dropped into a cardboard box under the table. There was a massive jumble of them in place now.

Some would never be missed. Figuring that the top layer had to be the most recent records, Alvirah scooped up an armful and stuffed them in her voluminous handbag. She delivered three more orders to the bar between eleven and twelve. In between deliveries, unable to stand the grimy kitchen, she set about cleaning it up as a bemused Hank watched.

After a quick stop at the Port Authority to change into her good clothes, scrub the rouge and purple shadow from her face, and wrap a turban around her flaming hair, Alvirah stepped out of a cab at quarter of one. Ramon, the night doorman, said, 'Sister Cordelia was here. She asked a lot of questions about where you were.'

Cordelia was no dope, Alvirah thought with grudging praise. But a plan was forming in her mind and Cordelia was part of it.

Even before she sank her tired body into the Jacuzzi that was bubbling with Cypress Point Spa oils, Alvirah sorted out the greasy order slips. Within the hour she had narrowed the possibilities. Seven rooms consistently sent for large orders. She pushed away the gnawing fear that they were all occupied by card players or some other kind of gamblers and that Willy might be in Alaska right now. Her instinct had told her the minute she set foot in the hotel that he was nearby.

It was nearly three when she got into the double

bed. Tired as she was it was impossible to get to sleep. Finally she pictured him there, settling in beside her. 'Nighty-night, Willy, lovey,' she said aloud and in her head heard him saying, 'Sleep tight, honey.'

On Thursday morning Clarence's eyes were crossing with the crushing ache that was splitting his head from ear to ear. Even Tony was careful not to cross him. He didn't reach for the television but contented himself sitting next to Willy and in a hoarse whisper telling him the story of his life. He'd gotten up to age seven, the year he'd discovered how easy it was to shoplift in the candy store when Clarence barked from the bed, 'You say you can fix that damn leak?'

Willy didn't want to seem too excited but the muscles in his throat squeezed together as he nodded vigorously.

'Whaddaya need?'

'A monkey wrench,' Willy croaked through the gag. 'A screwdriver. Wire.'

'All right. Sammy, you heard him. Go out and get that stuff.'

Sammy was playing solitaire again. 'I'll send Tony.'

Clarence bolted up. 'I said YOU. That dopey brother of yours'll blab to the nearest guy where he's going, why he's going, who he's getting it for. Now go.'

Sammy shivered at the tone, remembering how Tony had gone joyriding in the getaway car. 'Sure, Clarence, sure,' he said soothingly. 'And listen, long as I'm out, why not bring in some Chinese food, huh? Could taste good for a change.'

Clarence's scowl faded momentarily. 'Yeah, okay. Get lotsa soy sauce.'

Sister Cordelia arrived at seven o'clock on Thursday morning. Alvirah was prepared for her. She'd been up half an hour and was wearing Willy's plaid bathrobe, which had the faint scent of his shaving lotion and a pot of coffee on the stove. 'What's up?' Cordelia asked abruptly.

Over coffee and Sara Lee crumbcake Alvirah explained. 'Cordelia,' she concluded, 'I won't tell you I'm not scared because that would be a lie. I'm scared to death for Willy. But if someone is watching this place or maybe has a delivery boy keeping an eye out and it gets back that strange people were coming and going, they'll kill Willy. Cordelia, I swear to you he's in that hotel and I have a plan. Maeve still has her gun permit, doesn't she?'

'Yes.' Sister Cordelia's piercing gray eyes bored into Alvirah's face.

'And she's still friends with the guys she sent to prison, isn't she?'

'Oh sure. They all love her. You know they give Willy a hand fixing pipes whenever he needs it and they take turns delivering meals to our shut-ins.'

'That's what I mean. They look like the people who hand out in that place. I want three or four of them to check into the Lincoln Arms tonight. Let them get a card game going. That happens all the time. Tomorrow night at seven o'clock, I get the call where to leave the money. They know that I won't turn it over until I talk to Willy. They can't carry him out of there so I want Maeve's guys covering the exits. It's our only chance.'

Cordelia stared grimly into space, then said, 'Alvirah, Willy always told me to trust your sixth sense. I guess I'd better do it now.'

The chow mein was a welcome relief from the hamburgers. After dinner, Clarence ordered Willy to go into the John and get rid of the dripping noise. Sammy accompanied him. Willy's heart sank when Sammy said, 'I don't know how to fix nothing, but I know how not to fix it so don't get smart.'

So much for my big plan, Willy thought. Well, maybe I can stall it till I figure something out. He began by chipping at the years of accumulated rust around the base of the tank.

Alvirah dropped off the suitcase with her last bank pick-up at twenty to four, barely time enough to rush to the Port Authority, change, and report to the job. As she trotted through the Lincoln Arms lobby she noticed a sweet-faced nun in traditional habit holding out a basket and quietly moving from one to the other occupants of the bar. Everybody threw something in. In the kitchen, Alvirah asked Hank about the nun.

'Oh her. Yeah. She spends it on the kids who live around here. Makes everybody feel good to toss her a buck or two. Kind of spiritual, you know what I mean.'

That night deliveries were not as brisk as the night before. Alvirah suggested to Hank that she sort out all the old slips in the order box.

'Why?' Hank looked astonished.

Alvirah tugged at the sweatshirt she was wearing today. It said, 'I spent the night with Burt Reynolds'. Willy had bought it as a gag when they went to Reynold's theater in Florida. She tried to look mysterious. Why would anybody sort out useless slips? 'You never know,' she whispered.

The answer seemed to satisfy Hank.

She hid the already sorted slips under the pile she dumped on the table. She already knew what she was looking for. Consistent orders in quantity since Monday.

She narrowed it down to the same four rooms she'd selected at home.

At six o'clock it suddenly got busy. By eight-thirty

she'd delivered to three of the four suspect rooms. Two were the ongoing card games. One was now a crap game. She had to admit that none of the players looked like kidnappers.

Room 802 did not phone for an order. Maybe the guy with the bad headache and his brother had checked out. At midnight a discouraged Alvirah was about to leave when Hank grumbled, 'Working with you is easy. The new day guy quit and tomorrow they're gonna bring in the kid who fills in. He screws up all the orders.'

Breathing a grateful prayer of thanks Alvirah immediately volunteered to come in for the morning shift of seven to one as well as her usual four to twelve. She reasoned that she could still rush to the banks, which had promised to have cash between twelve-fifteen and three.

'I'll be back at seven,' she promised Hank.

'So will I,' he complained. 'The day cook quit, too.'

On the way out Alvirah noticed some familiar faces hanging around the bar. Louie, who'd served seven years for bankrobbery and had a black belt in karate; Al, who'd been a strongman for a pawnbroker and served four years for assault; Lefty, whose specialty was hot cars.

True to their training, even though Alvirah was sure they'd seen her, neither Louie, Al, nor Lefty gave any sign of knowing her.

Willy reduced the dripping to it's original annoying level then an irritable Clarence shouted in for him to knock off the hammering. 'I can put up with that noise for another twenty-four hours.'

And then what, Willy wondered. There was one hope. Sammy was bored with observing him fiddling around with the water tank. Tomorrow Sammy would be more careless. That night Willy insured the further need of his services by again crawling over to the watertank and adjusting the drip-drip level.

In the morning Sammy's eyes were feverish. Tony started talking about an old girlfriend he planned to look up when they got to the hide-out in Queens and no one told him to keep his mouth shut. Meaning, Willy thought, they're not worried about me hearing them.

When breakfast was delivered, Willy, securely stashed in the closet, jumped so suddenly that the gun in Sammy's hand almost went off. This time he didn't hear just a cadence of a voice that reminded him of Alvirah. It was her ringing tone asking Herman if his brother's headache was any better.

A startled Sammy hissed in Willy's ear, 'You crazy or somethin'?'

Alvirah was looking for him. Willy had to help her. He had to get back into the bathroom, work on the water tank, and tap the wrench to the tune of 'Casey Would Waltz with the Strawberry Blonde', the song they were playing when he first asked Alvirah to dance at the K of C hall over forty years ago.

He got his chance four hours later when, wrench and screwdriver in hand, a jittery Sammy beside him, at Clarence's furious command, he resumed his task of jointly fixing and sabotaging the water tank.

He was careful not to overdo. He reasonably told a protesting Sammy that he wasn't making that much noise, and anyway, this place would probably love to have one decent john. Scratching his four-day growth of beard, squirming in his wrinkled clothing, Willy began to send off signals three minutes apart, tap/TAP/taaap/tap – 'and the band played on'.

Alvirah was delivering pizzas to 702 when she heard it. The tapping. Oh God, she prayed, Oh God. She placed the tray on the uneven tabletop. The occupant of the room, a nice looking fellow in his thirties, was coming off a binge. He pointed up. 'Wouldn't that kill you? They're renovating or something. Take your pick. Sounds like Niagara Falls or New Year's Eve up there.'

'It has to be 802,' Alvirah decided, thinking of the guy on the bed, the doorkeeper, the open bathroom. They must shove Willy in the closet when they order room service. Even though she was so excited her heart was thumping through the sweatshirt that read, 'Don't be a litterbug', she took time to caution the drinker that booze would be his ruination.

There was a phone in the hallway by the bar. Hoping she wasn't being observed by the desk clerk, Alvirah made a hurried call to Cordelia. She finished by saying, 'They'll be phoning me at seven o'clock.'

At quarter of seven that night, the occupants of the bar of the Lincoln Arms Hotel were awed at the sight of eight mostly elderly nuns, in traditional floor-length habits, veils, and wimples, entering the lobby softly humming a hymn about the River Jordan. The desk clerk jumped up and made a shooing motion toward the revolving door behind them. Alvirah watched, tray in arms, as Maeve, the appointed spokesman stared down the desk clerk.

'We have the owner's permission to sing a concert on every floor and ask for donations,' Maeve told him.

'You got no such thing.'

Her voice dropped to a whisper. 'We have Mr . . .'s permission.'

The clerk's face paled. 'You guys shut up and get out your loot,' he yelled at the occupants of the bar. 'These here sisters are gonna sing hymns for ya.'

'No, we're starting upstairs,' Maeve told him. 'We'll complete the concert here.'

Alvirah protectively brought up the rear as the bevy of nuns led by Cordelia entered the elevator singing, 'Michael row your boat ashore. Hallelujah.'

They went directly to the eighth floor and clustered in the hallway where Lefty, Al and Louie were waiting. At exactly seven o'clock Alvirah knocked on the door. 'Room service,' she called.

'We didn't order,' a voice snarled.

'Someone did and I've got to collect,' she shouted firmly.

She heard scuffling. A door slammed. The closet. They were hiding Willy. The door opened a crack. A nervous Tony instructed, 'Leave the tray outside. How much?'

Alvirah kept her foot firmly in the door as strains of 'Michael, row your boat ashore' filled the corridor. The oldest nuns materialized behind Alvirah. Clarence had the phone in his hand. 'Shut up out there,' he shouted.

'Hey, that's no way to talk to the sisters,' Tony protested. Reverently he stood aside as they drifted past him into the room.

Sister Maeve brought up the rear, her hands folded in the sleeves of her gown. In an instant, she circled behind Clarence, yanked her right hand out and held a gun against his temple. In the crisp tone that had made her a superb cop, she whispered, 'Freeze, or you're dead.'

Tony opened his mouth to yell a warning, but it was obliterated by several loud hallelujah's as Lefty karated him into unconsciousness. Lefty then insured Clarence's silence with a judicious rap on the neck that made him collapse beside Tony on the floor.

Louie and Al herded the reluctant Sister Cordelia and her elderly flock into the safety of the hallway. It was time to rescue Willy. Lefty had his hand ready to

200

strike. Sister Maeve had her gun pointed. Alvirah threw open the closet door as she bellowed, 'Room service'.

Sammy was standing next to Willy, his gun in Willy's neck. 'Outside, all of you,' he snarled. 'Drop that gun, lady.'

Maeve hesitated, then obeyed.

Sammy released the safety catch on the revolver.

He's trapped and he's desperate, Alvirah thought frantically. He's going to kill my Willy. She forced herself to sound calm. 'I've got a car in front of the hotel,' she told him. 'There's two million dollars in it. Take Willy and me with you. You can check the money, drive away and then let us out somewhere.' She turned to Lefty and Maeve, 'Don't try to stop us or he'll hurt Willy. Get lost all of you.' She held her breath and stared at Willy's captor willing herself to seem confident.

Sammy hesitated for an instant. Alvirah watched as he turned the gun to point at the door. 'It better be there, lady,' he snapped. 'Untie his feet.'

Obediently she knelt down and yanked at the knots binding Willy's ankles. She peeked up as she undid the last one. The gun was still pointed at the door. Alvirah remembered how she used to put her shoulder under Mrs. O'Keefe's piano and hoist it up to straighten the carpet. One, two, three. She shot up like an arrow, her shoulder whamming into Sammy's gun hand. He pulled the trigger as he dropped the gun. The bullet released flaking paint from the drooping ceiling.

Willy threw his manacled hands around Sammy, bearhugging him until the others rushed back into the room.

As though in a dream, Alvirah watched Lefty, Al and Louie free Willy from his handcuffs and ropes and

201

use them to secure the abductors. She heard Maeve dial 911 and say, 'This is Officer Maeve O'Reilly, I mean Sister Maeve Marie reporting a kidnapping, attempted murder and successful apprehension of the perpetrators.'

Alvirah felt Willy's arms around her. 'Hi, honey,' he whispered.

She was so filled with joy that she couldn't speak. They gazed at each other. She took in his bloodshot eyes, stubble of beard and matted hair. He studied her garish makeup and 'Don't be a litterbug' sweatshirt. 'Honey, you're gorgeous,' Willy said fervently. 'I'm sorry if I look like one of the Smith brothers.'

Alvirah rubbed her face against his. The tears of relief that were welling in her throat vanished as she began to laugh. 'Oh, sweetie,' she cried, 'you'll always look like Tip O'Neill to me.'

I'll Be Seeing You

A Novel By
Mary Higgins Clark

Available in Paperback from Arrow

The following pages are taken from
the opening chapters of the novel.

I'll Be Seeing You

CHAPTER 1

Meghan Collins stood somewhat aside from the cluster of other journalists in Emergency at Manhattan's Roosevelt Hospital. Minutes before, a retired United States senator had been mugged on Central Park West and rushed here. The media were milling around, awaiting word of his condition.

Meghan lowered her heavy tote bag to the floor. The wireless mike, cellular telephone and notebooks were causing the strap to dig into her shoulder blade. She leaned against the wall and closed her eyes for a moment's rest. All the reporters were tired. They'd been in court since early afternoon, awaiting the verdict in a fraud trial. At nine o'clock, just as they were leaving, the call came to cover the mugging. It was now nearly eleven. The crisp October day had turned into an overcast night that was an unwelcome promise of an early winter.

It was a busy night in the hospital. Young parents carrying a bleeding toddler were waved past the registration desk through the door to the examination area. Bruised and shaken passengers of a car accident consoled each other as they awaited medical treatment.

Outside, the persistent wail of arriving and departing ambulances added to the familiar cacophony of New York traffic.

A hand touched Meghan's arm. 'How's it going, Counselor?'

It was Jack Murphy from Channel 5. His wife had gone through NYU Law School with Meghan. Unlike Meghan, however, Liz was practicing law. Meghan Collins, Juris Doctor, had worked for a Park Avenue law firm for six months, quit and got a job at WPCD radio as a news reporter. She'd been there three years now and for the past month had been borrowed regularly by PCD Channel 3, the television affiliate.

'It's going okay, I guess,' Meghan told him. Her beeper sounded.

'Have dinner with us soon,' Jack said. 'It's been too long.' He rejoined his cameraman as she reached to get her cellular phone out of the bag.

The call was from Ken Simon at the WPCD radio news desk. 'Meg, the EMS scanner just picked up an ambulance heading for Roosevelt. Stabbing victim found on Fifty-sixth Street and Tenth. Watch for her.'

The ominous ee-aww sound of an approaching ambulance coincided with the staccato tapping of hurrying feet. The trauma team was heading for the Emergency entrance. Meg broke the connection, dropped the phone in her bag and followed the empty stretcher as it was wheeled out to the semicircular driveway.

The ambulance screeched to a halt. Experienced hands rushed to assist in transferring the victim to the stretcher. An oxygen mask was clamped on her face. The sheet covering her slender body was blood-stained. Tangled chestnut hair accentuated the blue-tinged pallor of her neck.

Meg rushed to the driver's door. 'Any witnesses?' she asked quickly.

'None came forward.' The driver's face was lined and weary, his voice matter-of-fact. 'There's an alley between two of those old tenements near Tenth. Looks like someone came up from behind, shoved her in it and stabbed her. Probably happened in a split second.'

'How bad is she?'

'As bad as you can get.'

'Identification?'

'None. She'd been robbed. Probably hit by some druggie who needed a fix.'

The stretcher was being wheeled in. Meghan darted back into the Emergency room behind it.

One of the reporters snapped, 'The senator's doctor is about to give a statement.'

The media surged across the room to crowd around the desk. Meghan did not know what instinct kept her near the stretcher. She watched as the doctor about to start an IV removed the oxygen mask and lifted the victim's eyelids.

'She's gone,' he said.

Meghan looked over a nurse's shoulder and stared down into the unseeing blue eyes of the dead young woman. She gasped as she took in those eyes, the broad forehead, arched brows, high cheekbones, straight nose, generous lips.

It was as though she was looking into a mirror.

She was looking at her own face.

CHAPTER 2

Meghan took a cab to her apartment in Battery Park City, at the very tip of Manhattan. It was an expensive fare, but it was late and she was very tired. By the time she arrived home, the numbing shock of seeing the dead woman was deepening rather than wearing off. The victim had been stabbed in the chest, possibly four to five hours before she was found. She'd been wearing jeans, a lined denim jacket, running shoes and socks. Robbery had probably been the motive. Her skin was tanned. Narrow bands of lighter skin on her wrist and several fingers suggested that rings and a watch were missing. Her pockets were empty and no handbag was found.

Meghan switched on the foyer light and looked across the room. From her windows she could see Ellis Island and the Statue of Liberty. She could watch the cruise ships being piloted to their berths on the Hudson River. She loved downtown New York, the narrowness of the streets, the sweeping majesty of the World Trade Center, the bustle of the financial district.

The apartment was a good-sized studio with a sleeping alcove and kitchen unit. Meghan had furnished it with her mother's castoffs, intending eventually to get a larger place and gradually redecorate. In the three years she'd worked for WPCD that had not happened.

She tossed her coat over a chair, went into the bathroom and changed into pajamas and a robe. The apartment was pleasantly warm, but she felt chilled to the point of illness. She realized she was avoiding looking into the vanity mirror. Finally she turned and studied herself as she reached for the cleansing cream.

Her face was chalk white, her eyes staring. Her hands trembled as she released her hair so that it spilled around her neck.

In frozen disbelief she tried to pick out differences between herself and the dead woman. She remembered that the victim's face had been a little fuller, the shape of her eyes round rather than oval, her chin smaller. But the skin tone and the color of the hair and the open, unseeing eyes were so very like her own.

She knew where the victim was now. In the medical

examiner's morgue, being photographed and finger-printed. Dental charts would be made.

And then the autopsy.

Meghan realized she was trembling. She hurried into the kitchenette, opened the refrigerator and re-moved the carton of milk. Hot chocolate. Maybe that would help.

She settled on the couch and hugged her knees, the steaming cup in front of her. The phone rang. It was probably her mother, so she hoped her voice sounded steady when she answered it.

'Meg, hope you weren't asleep.'

'No, just got in. How's it going, Mom?'

'All right, I guess. I heard from the insurance people today. They're coming over tomorrow afternoon again. I hope to God they don't ask any more questions about that loan Dad took out on his policies. They can't seem to fathom that I have no idea what he did with the money.'

In late January, Meghan's father had been driving home to Connecticut from Newark Airport. It had been snowing and sleeting all day. At seven-twenty, Edwin Collins made a call from his car phone to a business associate, Victor Orsini, to set up a meeting the next morning. He told Orsini he was on the approach to the Tappan Zee Bridge.

In what may have been only a few seconds later, a fuel tanker spun out of control on the bridge and crashed into a tractor trailer, causing a series of ex-plosions and a fireball that engulfed seven or eight automobiles. The tractor trailer smashed into the side of the bridge and tore open a gaping hole before plunging into the swirling, icy waters of the Hudson River. The fuel tanker followed, dragging with it the other disintegrating vehicles.

A badly injured eyewitness who'd managed to steer

out of the direct path of the fuel tanker testified that a dark blue Cadillac sedan spun out in front of him and disappeared through the gaping steel. Edwin Collins had been driving a dark blue Cadillac.

It was the worst disaster in the history of the bridge. Eight lives were lost. Meg's sixty-year-old father never made it home that night. He was assumed to have died in the explosion. The New York Thruway authorities were still searching for scraps of wreckage and bodies, but now, nearly nine months later, no trace had as yet been found of either him or his car.

A memorial mass had been offered a week after the accident, but because no death certificate had been issued, Edwin and Catherine Collins' joint assets were frozen and the large insurance policies on his life had not been paid.

Bad enough for Mom to be heartbroken without the hassle these people are giving her, Meg thought. 'I'll be up tomorrow afternoon, Mom. If they keep stalling, we may have to file suit.'

She debated, then decided that the last thing her mother needed was to hear that a woman with a striking resemblance to Meghan had been stabbed to death. Instead she talked about the trial she'd covered that day.

For a long time, Meghan lay in bed, dozing fitfully. Finally she fell into a deep sleep.

A high-pitched squeal pulled her awake. The fax began to whine. She looked at the clock: it was quarter-past four. What on earth? she thought.

She switched on the light, pulled herself up on one elbow and watched as paper slowly slid from the machine. She jumped out of bed, ran across the room and reached for the message.

It read: MISTAKE. ANNIE WAS A MISTAKE.

CHAPTER 3

Tom Weicker, fifty-two-year-old news director of PCD Channel 3, had been borrowing Meghan Collins from the radio affiliate with increasing frequency. He was in the process of handpicking another reporter for the on-air news team and had been rotating the candidates, but now he had made his final decision: Meghan Collins.

He reasoned that she had good delivery, could ad lib at the drop of a hat and always gave a sense of immediacy and excitement to even a minor news item. Her legal training was a real plus at trials. She was damn good-looking and had natural warmth. She liked people and could relate to them.

On Friday morning, Weicker sent for Meghan. When she knocked at the open door of his office, he waved her in. Meghan was wearing a fitted jacket in tones of pale blue and rust brown. A skirt in the same fine wool skimmed the top of her boots. Classy, Weicker thought, perfect for the job.

Meghan studied Weicker's expression, trying to read his thoughts. He had a thin, sharp-featured face and wore rimless glasses. That and his thinning hair made him look older than his age and more like a bank teller than a media powerhouse. It was an impression quickly dispelled, however, when he began to speak. Meghan liked Tom but knew that his nickname, 'Lethal Weicker', had been earned. When he began borrowing her from the radio station he'd made it clear that it was a tough, lousy break that her father had lost his life in the bridge tragedy, but he needed her reassurance that it wouldn't affect her job performance.

It hadn't, and now Meghan heard herself being offered the job she wanted so badly.

The immediate, reflexive reaction that flooded through her was, I can't wait to tell Dad!

Thirty floors below, in the garage of the PCD building, Bernie Heffernan, the parking attendant, was in Tom Weicker's car, going through the glove compartment. By some genetic irony, Bernie's features had been formed to give him the countenance of a merry soul. His cheeks were plumb, his chin and mouth small, his eyes wide and guileless, his hair thick and rumpled, his body sturdy, if somewhat rotund. At thirty-five the immediate impression he gave to observers was that he was a guy who, though wearing his best suit, would fix your flat tire.

He still lived with his mother in the shabby house in Jackson Heights, Queens, where he'd been born. The only times he'd been away from it were those dark, nightmarish periods when he was incarcerated. The day after his twelfth birthday he was sent to a juvenile detention center for the first of a dozen times. In his early twenties he'd spent three years in a psychiatric facility. Four years ago he was sentenced to ten months in Riker's Island. That was when the police caught him hiding in a college student's car. He'd been warned a dozen times to stay away from her. Funny, Bernie thought – he couldn't even remember what she looked like now. Not her and not any of them. And they had all been so important to him at the time.

Bernie never wanted to go to jail again. The other inmates frightened him. Twice they beat him up. He has sworn to Mama that he'd never hide in shrubs and look in windows again, or follow a woman and try to kiss her. He was getting very good at controlling his temper too. He'd hated the psychiatrist who kept warning Mama that one day that vicious temper

212

would get Bernie into trouble no one could fix. Bernie knew that nobody had to worry about him anymore.

His father had taken off when he was a baby. His embittered mother no longer ventured outside, and at home Bernie had to endure her incessant reminders of all the inequities life had inflicted on her during her seventy-three years and how much he owed her.

Well, whatever he 'owed' her, Bernie managed to spend most of his money on electronic equipment. He had a radio that scanned police calls, another radio powerful enough to receive programs from all over the world, a voice-altering device.

At night he dutifully watched television with his mother. After she went to bed at ten o'clock, however, Bernie snapped off the television, rushed down to the basement, turned on the radios and began to call talk show hosts. He made up names and backgrounds to give them. He'd call a right-wing host and rant liberal values, a liberal host and sing the praises of the extreme right. In his call-in persona, he loved arguments, confrontations, trading insults.

Unknown to his mother he also had a forty-inch television and a VCR in the basement and often watched movies he had brought home from porn shops.

The police scanner inspired other ideas. He began to go through telephone books and circle numbers that were listed in women's names. He would dial one of those numbers in the middle of the night and say he was calling from a cellular phone outside her home and was about to break in. He'd whisper that maybe he'd just pay a visit, or maybe he'd kill her. Then Bernie would sit and chuckle as he listened to the police scanners sending a squad car rushing to the address. It was almost as good as peeking in windows or following women, and he never had to worry about the headlights of a police car suddenly shining on him, or a cop on a loudspeaker yelling, 'Freeze'.

The car belonging to Tom Weicker was a gold mine of information for Bernie. Weicker had an electronic address book in the glove compartment. In it he kept the names, addresses and numbers of the key staff of the station. The big shots, Bernie thought, as he copied numbers on to his own electronic pad. He'd even reached Weicker's wife at home one night. She had begun to shriek when he told her he was at the back door and on his way in.

Afterwards, recalling her terror, he'd giggled for hours.

What was getting hard for him now was that for the first time since he was released from Riker's Island, he had that scary feeling of not being able to get someone out of his mind. This one was a reporter. She was so pretty that when he opened the car door for her it was a struggle not to touch her.

Her name was Meghan Collins.

BESTSELLERS FROM ARROW

by Mary Higgins Clark

WHILE MY PRETTY ONE SLEEPS

A superbly compelling story of chilling mystery set against the glittering world of New York's fashion industry.

Ethel Lambston, gossip writer, is known to many but loved by few. Her sudden disappearance triggers the concern of Neeve Kearny, owner of the boutique where Ethel shopped. Neeve soon finds herself in danger, haunted by the feeling that she knows the clue to the murder, but unaware that the killer is closer than she could ever have imagined . . .

'Clark can prickle scalps with shivery skill'

COSMOPOLITAN

'A master at capturing the suspense lurking behind the façade of ordinary life'

LITERARY GUILD

THE ANASTASIA SYNDROME

Trapped in her seventeenth-century past, a brilliant writer exacts an ancient revenge in the twentieth . . . a child wanders, lost and alone, in the maze of New York . . . a lottery ticket flips up a winning combination of love and violent death . . . an unsuccessful actor hopes for a breakthrough with his chilling new role . . . a class reunion offers fulfilment of a schoolboy crush . . .

Four miniature masterpieces of tension, and a novella of obsession and possession, confirm Mary Higgins Clark as a spellbinding storyteller – the Queen of romantic suspense.

'There is no one quite like Mary Higgins Clark when it comes to mystery and suspense'
BARBARA TAYLOR BRADFORD

LOVES MUSIC, LOVES TO DANCE

'As spine-chilling as anything else I have read'
OPTIONS

Erin and Darcy, answering personal ads as research for a TV show, discover a whole New York subculture – adulterers, con men, the shy and frankly weird, all looking for love. And one man looking for something darker . . .

A serial killer who has got away with murder for fifteen years, and has promised himself just two more . . .

'Brilliant, nail-biting, shock-horror stuff . . . Original, fast-paced, and absolutely unputdownable'
NEW WOMAN

'The throat-clutching dénouement is pure Clark – inevitable, horrible and, ultimately, irresistible'
PEOPLE

'Oozes tension from the very first page. Gripping'
BOOKWORLD

ALL AROUND THE TOWN

'The alter-ego psychology is intriguing'
SUNDAY EXPRESS

When Allan Grant is found stabbed to death, Laurie Kenyon's fingerprints abound . . .

To cope with the trauma Laurie suffered after she was kidnapped for two years at the age of four, she has developed a multiple personality. The real Laurie has no recollection of the shocking murder.

The key to Laurie's innocence lies in what happened during her two years of hell. Bic Hawkins, and his wife Opal, Laurie's abductors, are now prominent television evangelists. Bic had threatened Laurie with death if she talked – a threat he may have to carry out . . .

'A psychological thriller that's so gripping you won't want to put it down for an instant'
WOMAN AND HOME

'Tautly-written psychological suspense which will keep you awake at night'
ANNABEL

Also in Arrow

THE MAN WHO LIED TO WOMEN

Carol O'Connell

Fifteen years after Inspector Louis Markowitz adopted the wild child, no one in the New York's Special Crimes section knew much about Kathy Mallory's origins. They only knew that the young cop with the soul of a thief could bewitch the most complex computer systems, could slip into the minds of killers with disturbing ease.

In Central Park, a woman dies, while a witness watches, believing the brutal murder to be a prelude to a kiss. Mallory goes hunting the killer, armed with under-the-skin knowledge of the man's mind and the bare clue of a lie.

Mallory holds on to one truth: everybody lies, and some lies can get you killed. And she knows that, to trap the killer, she must put her own life at risk, for this killer has taken a personal interest in her . . .

'Mallory's progress is enthralling . . . beautifully observed in fine, controlled prose'
Mail on Sunday

'Carol O'Connell is a gifted writer with a style as quick and arresting as Kathy Mallory herself'
Richard North Patterson

JAMAICA INN

Daphne du Maurier

Stark and forbidding, Jamaica Inn stands alone on bleak Bodmin Moor, its very walls tainted with corruption. Young Mary Yellan soon learns of her uncle Joss Merlyn's strange trade here – but does he deal in blacker secrets still?

As her suspicions and her terror increase, she looks in vain for help from the fearful Cornish people. Only in the Vicar of Altarnun does she find a friend – and in the oddly likeable horse-thief they call the worst Merlyn of them all . . .

And, as the drama in this famous gothic masterpiece heightens, Mary must choose which to trust.

THE RENDEZVOUS AND OTHER STORIES

Daphne du Maurier

The Rendezvous and Other Stories spans the whole of Daphne du Maurier's writing career, during which time 'something observed, something said, would sink into the hidden places of my mind and a story would form'.

'A real through-the-night read . . . the most brilliant collection of her stories yet'
Cosmopolitan

'The philanderer playing all the odds, the private detective pursuing a mystery he'll have to keep to himself, the famous actor saving his best performance for an admirer he can't recall, a weekend in Paris that goes disastrously wrong – crisply told and neatly pointed'
Oxford Times

'Superb . . . fourteen tales touched by the haunting quality which has always distinguished her work'
Annabel

THE HOUSE ON THE STRAND

Daphne du Maurier

At a crossroads in his life, Dick Young agrees to experiment with a new drug his friend Magnus is developing – a drug that offers an extraordinary escape route from his own unsatisfactory world.

Transported to the fourteenth century, Dick witnesses the vivid life of the Cornish manor of Tywardreath: its intrigues, adulteries and violent deaths seen through the eyes of the strangely compelling Roger. Increasingly obsessed by Roger and the magnetic Isolda Carminowe, he resents more and more the time he must spend in the modern world . . .

Despite Magnus's warnings and the shocking example of the tragedy, Dick escapes more often and more recklessly into this other reality – and, in a final, defiant risk, throws his whole life into the balance.

MALLORY'S ORACLE

Carol O'Connell

When Kathleen Mallory was ten she was a street kid and a thief. Then a cop called Markowitz took her home to his wife to civilize her . . .

Now Mallory is in charge of a complex database and a police officer herself, and someone has just murdered the man she considers her father – the only man she has ever loved.

More used to the company of computers than people, Mallory descends into the urban nightmare of New York, to hunt down a cold-blooded killer.

Mallory's Oracle is a dangerous chase through the city's underworld, down the fibre-optic cables of hi-tech computer networks and behind the blinds of genteel Gramercy Park – and an investigation into the chilly heart of its damaged and elusive heroine.

'A cracking good thriller'
Sunday Express

'Something close to a masterwork'
The Times

'Sgt Kathleen Mallory is one of the most original and intriguing detectives you'll ever meet'
Carl Hiaasen

'A stunning debut'
Daily Mirror

'A deeply satisfying read'
Time Out

Buy *Clark*

Order further *Mary Higgins Clark* titles
from your local bookshop, or have them
delivered direct to your door by Bookpost

FREE POST AND PACKING

Overseas customers allow £2 per paperback

PHONE: 01624 677237

POST: Random House Books
c/o Bookpost, PO Box 29, Douglas
Isle of Man, IM99 1BQ

FAX: 01624 670923

EMAIL: bookshop@enterprise.net

Cheques (payable to Bookpost) and credit
cards accepted

Prices and availability subject to change without notice
Allow 28 days for delivery
When placing your order, please state if you do not wish to receive
any additional information.

www.randomhouse.co.uk